A Holly jolly Christmas

A Lesbian Christmas Romcom

Emily Wright

A HOLLY JOLLY CHRISTMAS

Copyright © 2023 by Emily Wright.

Warnings: This book contains sexually explicit material which is only suitable for mature readers.

For information contact:

Purple Clouds Press

www.purplecloudspress.co.uk

Emily Wright

www.emilywrightwriter.co.uk

Book and Cover design by Mitxeran

Published by Purple Clouds Press

ISBN: 978-1-7395624-1-0

First Edition: November 2023

Subscribe to my newsletter to stay in touch and also receive a free sapphic novella!

www.emilywrightwriter.co.uk/contact

"The risk of love is loss, and the price of loss is grief—but the pain of grief is only a shadow when compared with never risking love."

—— Hilary Stanton Zuni

Chapter One

If I was to take anything as a sign not to return home for Christmas, being shat on by a scabby, bloated pigeon would do the trick. Anyone stupid enough to say it was good luck had clearly never been crapped on by a flying dustbin with feathers.

I pressed my lips together, cursing the bird for staining my black shearling coat. *Merry bloody Christmas to you, too, pigeon. Hope you choke on a mince pie.*

I ducked back into the comfort of my BMW and fumbled in the glove box. Brushing aside a handful of KitKat wrappers—Dani's no doubt, she always left my car in a state—I found a pack of tissues and got to work scrubbing the faeces.

A car horn blared, and I nearly gave myself

whiplash. In the rearview mirror, a steady queue of vehicles waited behind me for the petrol pump. *Oops.* I scrambled to put the car in drive, held up a hand in apology, and pulled into an empty parking space facing the fast food place opposite.

Kids were rushing through the automatic doors, pulling tired parents behind them. It was the time of year for bribing children for good behaviour. My dad would do the same with me and my brother whenever he took us shopping. No fighting and no arguing meant we could get a kiddy meal each on the way home—as long as we didn't tell Mum, of course. She hated fast food, thought it was a first-class ticket to childhood obesity. Judging by the oversized pigeon-poop dispensers pecking at burger remains in the car park, she wasn't too far wrong.

My fingers twitched for my phone. The urge to text Cameron still floored me daily. Like a high-speed train ploughing straight through my chest. I scrunched the tissue and threw it onto the passenger's seat. He'd have loved this, me getting shat on. I missed his laugh. It was kind of goofy, but you couldn't help but laugh with him. He was contagious like that. Always the brightest person in the room. Used to be.

I reached for my phone anyway and selected his name, ignoring the plethora of previously unanswered messages, and began to type.

I'm doing it, Cam. I'm really doing it this time. I

promised you I would, but it's hard. I know you'd laugh at me and tell me to get over myself. It's only home, after all. But it doesn't feel like it without you there.

I sent the message and received the rebound text immediately; no time to duck the high-speed train. I swallowed the lump in my throat, then put my phone back in its holder and laid my head against the cool leather of the steering wheel.

The urge to turn the car around grew stronger. But I wanted to do this. I had to.

"Hey, Zoodle, call Dani," I mumbled.

"Calling: Bill the Postman."

I sat up. "No, no! Zoodle, stop! Call DA-NI."

The lights flickered on the dashboard. *"Calling: Katie."*

I jabbed the end call button with my finger, almost breaking my freshly painted nails. My ex was the absolute last person I wanted to speak to. I manually selected Dani's name and waited for her to pick up.

On the fourth ring, she answered. "Missing me already?"

"Remind me why I'm doing this again, please?"

"Because if you don't, I'll kick your ass."

I snorted, imagining the barely five-foot woman being violent. She had a feisty streak—there was no denying that—but in the two years I'd known her, the most threatening thing I'd seen her do was evict spiders from the office via the window. She liked to think she'd inherited some of the ruthless genes from her professional boxer dad. In reality, she was the equivalent of a curly-haired Care Bear filled with jellybeans.

"I'm not joking, Holly Bradfield," she continued, "if you come back here, I'm going to give you the biggest wedgie ever recorded."

I laughed, already feeling better. "Pfft. You couldn't even reach the top of my knickers."

"Hey! I thought we agreed height jokes were off the table for the holidays. You owe me some chocolate."

"Yeah, you're right, I'm sorry. Which reminds me…This secret stash of KitKat wrappers in my car. Happen to know anything about that?"

She was quiet for a few moments, and then we both burst out laughing.

"I'm sorry, Hol, this dieting malarkey is no fun. I have to snack where no one can see me."

Dani had joined up with some other women in the office with the goal of losing a few pounds for Christmas. If one of them broke their "pact", she had to pay a fine. Unnecessary torture if you asked me, especially when it was meant to be a bit of fun, but Dani was very competitive.

"I told you, you don't need to lose any weight, Dani. You look great."

"And I told you, no turning back this year. It's time,

Holly. You need to see your family, you told me so yourself. And you'll be back on the twenty-sixth. The week will fly."

Her sudden seriousness struck a chord, vibrating the mix of anxiety, fear, and guilt into a swirl in my stomach.

"Are you sure you don't want me to come with you? I can get the next train up."

"No, no. It's fine. You've got your plans with Brandon. I'll be fine."

She sighed, crackling the speakers. "I know this is hard, but it's Christmas. I will not have you working in the office this year—it's just too sad. Plus, you're single again, so there's no excuse this time. The offer is there if you change your mind. I'm here for you, okay?"

I smiled. "Thanks, Dani. I appreciate it."

"You better. I'm missing *RuPaul's Drag Race* for this."

We both laughed, and the waves of sickness calmed in my gut. "Well, I shouldn't keep you then."

"You've got this, Hol. I love you!"

"I love you too."

I hung up, feeling refreshed and determined. I could do this. Going home for Christmas was supposed to be a good thing.

But it doesn't usually involve being chased by ghosts. And I wasn't in the mood for a low-budget remake of *A Christmas Carol* either. I'd enough shit to deal with without having to relive the most miserable moments of my life. I didn't need any help being reminded of those.

Vicky Castleton's face popped into my mind uninvited, just like it always did whenever I thought about going home. I had a feeling this trip might uncover more apparitions hiding in my closets than I cared to admit— not that I'd been in one of those for a few years.

I picked the scrunched-up pigeon-poo tissue off the seat and put it into the bin outside, along with Dani's KitKat wrappers. Then I shifted the car into drive and pulled out into the crisp December night. Dani was right; I could do this. I was finally going home.

Chapter Two

Dani was wrong. I couldn't do this. How could I go home and show my face after two years of hiding away? Well, not hiding away, but...not wanting to metaphorically scream *here I am, grief, come and find me.*

Grief lurked ominously in the darkness, behind every bend as the roads merged from motorway to country lane. It flashed in the rapid blinking lights of the petrol station on the corner, blinding me with their obnoxiously happy Christmas spirit. My car manoeuvred automatically, through the dodgy dips and the endless potholes that were never fixed, even now. Memories bombarded me as I passed familiar places. The lights still flickered by the park, where Cameron and I had our first swigs of cider on a freezing October night. It tasted like cat piss and looked like it too. We'd laughed about it all the way home, worrying that our parents would be able to smell it on our breath.

I rounded the corner to our street, indicating left and trying not to look at the teenagers at the bus stop. We used to sit there sometimes when there was nothing to do, filling each other in on school gossip. Cameron was in the year above me, but our friends all knew each other. He even set me up with one of his friends—Billy, a wannabe celebrity at school with his blond curly hair and strong swimmer's physique. We only went out for a few weeks before he dumped me for someone else, but Cameron held me at the bus stop until I'd finished crying. He also pulled Billy's trousers down at one of the swim meets for me and stopped being friends with him; it had been all people could talk about for weeks. He always had my back.

I drove up my street, guided by the luminous lights. The Smiths had a giant blow-up Father Christmas outside their house, waving half-heartedly at me in encouragement. All the houses looked the same as when I was a kid: the Kents, the Booths, the adorable elderly Jacksons on the end. People didn't tend to move around much here. A village like Mistleberry ensnared people, for better or for worse. There were no secrets. Everyone knew each other's business. It made for a sweet, tight-knit community, but neighbours also felt entitled to know every snippet of your personal life. There was nowhere to hide—unless you wanted to live among the sheep in the fields for the rest of your life…but Farmer Harry might not be too happy about that.

Our house—my house—waited at the top of the road, an insufferable "Santa Stop Here" sign flashing away in red and green. Dad's blue Fiat rested on the drive, Cameron's old Mini Cooper nowhere to be seen. For some reason, I'd hoped it would still be there, and disappointment washed over me. My heart ached at the thought of someone else driving it. Someone else rallying around the country lanes, singing old *Now That's What I Call Music* albums badly to the cows outside.

I pulled onto the kerb and shut off the engine. *Compose yourself, Holly. It's only Mum and Dad.* It wasn't as if I hadn't seen them. They'd visited my apartment in London, and we spoke on the phone often. It was just this place; there was too much to deal with.

I looked up at the houses in front of me, and a twinge of guilt rippled through my gut. Cameron's ghost wasn't the only one I'd be facing this week.

Victoria Castleton lived next door. Like most of the families here, they'd been in Mistleberry for generations. Our parents had been friends for years, and so when both my mum and Denise fell pregnant around the same time, a lifelong bond was formed.

Cameron, Vicky, and I would stay out in the fields behind our houses for hours, making dens and building rope-swings in the river. The older kids would tear them down, but we'd just build another.

Things changed when we got older. Vicky and I would laugh in our bedrooms for hours, making comic strips of the neighbours and the other kids we knew at school. We watched *Friends* on repeat, experimented with each other's hairstyles, and even did Cameron's make-up—it's safe to say that a pretty woman, he was not.

When Cameron got a girlfriend, Vicky and I teased him horrendously. But then something shifted, and I started to see her in a new light.

I'd hardly spoken to Vicky since my brother died, too lost in my own grief to have capacity for anyone else's. Our relationship had always been a little complicated, but I'd be lying if I said I never thought of her. Too many times I'd picked up my phone and typed a message, but I was too afraid of what she'd say. Too much time had passed. She'd probably moved anyway, and I had other things to think about. Like facing my parents after declaring this village a no-go zone for so long.

My insides squeezed, nausea clawing its way up my throat. I couldn't bear to see them upset. But I also couldn't bring myself to get out of the car.

Was I really back in Mistleberry? *What the hell am I doing?* I sucked in three deep breaths, trying to steady my shaking hands. What was I supposed to say? *"Sorry, Mum and Dad, for not coming to see you, but the very thought*

of being back in this village makes me want to vomit"?
Do I pretend nothing happened? Talk about Cameron?

My chest constricted as I forced air into my lungs.
Do I go inside or turn around?

I can't do this. I'm not ready.

A loud knock on the car window jolted me, snapping
my neck for the second time that evening. A shadowed
face hovered, its breath fogging up the glass.

"Holly? I thought that was you." The voice was
slightly muffled, and I was still none the wiser about
which snooping neighbour it belonged to.

The nosy shadow beckoned me outside with a wave
of its hand. *I guess this is it. I'm doing it. Oh, no.*

After a sigh, I forced myself from the safety of the
cushioned leather and out into the cold, crisp air. The
shadowed face shifted into shape as he backed away: the
big nose and greying beard of Mr Simon, who lived a few
doors down.

"Your mother said you were coming this year. When
the lights flashed past and Mabel meowed at the window,
I thought, it must be Holly...and it is!" He straightened
his jacket, even though it was already perfect, and
grinned, more wrinkles framing his mouth than I
remembered. "How are you, dear?"

Terrified? Nauseous? Cursing Dani for convincing
me this was a good idea? "I'm...fine, thank you, Mr
Simon. How are you?"

"Oh, well, you know how it is around here. My guttering fell off, so now the water drips and drips and…"

I nodded as he told me the very, very detailed story of all the woes in his life over the past two years. Cold seeped into my fingers and toes, chilling me to the core. I bounced in my shoes, trying to avoid frostbite.

"…then Mabel brought in yet another bird's head and this time—oh, no, dear, you're shivering! Do you want to come in for an eggnog? I also need some help with a Christmas tree, if you wouldn't mind. Or I could make you a cup of tea?"

And have a bird's head instead of a biscuit? No thanks, Jeff. "I'd b-b-better go say hi to the folks first. But another t-time."

"Righto, another time. I'll look forward to it!"

Great. Another hour of Jeff and Mabel's terrible adventures. "Sounds great!" Before he could start talking again, I heaved open the boot—which had already started to ice over—and pulled out my bag.

I didn't know what was worse—the sickness threatening to upheave itself or the cold threatening to snap my fingers off. Sadly, I could hardly leave now that Jeff had already seen me; that would only make matters of the family more complicated. Try explaining that one.

I waited awkwardly on the doorstep, cold spreading up my spine. Should I ring the bell? *Technically, it's my house…but then…it's been years.* I shifted my bag to my other shoulder, cursing Dani for insisting I bring an outfit for every occasion. There must've been bricks in there.

The door opened, the digital bell blaring and signifying my presence to the whole street. Under the light of the hallway, rounder and softer than I had seen him last, my dad looked up at me.

"Holly, you came."

Chapter Three

Dad's expression was unreadable. His nose was pinched in, like he was holding a sneeze, and his wiry ginger eyebrows twitched. Something flickered across his blue eyes. Disappointment? Surprise? His mouth opened, but no words came out. *Oh, god, please don't cry.*

"Shut the door, Alan, you're letting all the bloody cold in!" My mother's voice cut through Dad's momentary brain fart, and he stood aside.

Thrown off by Dad's unusual response, I shuffled past into the hallway, letting the familiarity wash over me. The same striped grey wallpaper that Mum insisted was "super modern, like Gok Wan" lined the walls. I'd tried to explain to her multiple times that Gok Wan was neither modern nor an interior designer, but the woman couldn't be deterred.

I placed my bag at the bottom of the stairs, avoiding the gallery of pictures depicting Cameron and me at various embarrassing states of childhood. How could they bear to look at these every day? A constant stab in the stomach every time you needed to go for a wee? No thanks.

With my boots off, I stood, aware of Dad's gaze wandering over my outfit.

"You look...different," he managed.

"So do you." I smiled, and he returned the gesture, something visibly relaxing in his face.

"I'm glad you came, Hol."

The tightness in my chest loosened too. Dad was alright. I just smiled again, hoping that was an adequate response.

"Come on, she's dying to see you." He turned to lead the way, like I hadn't walked this very hallway every day of my pre-adult life. The fact that Mum hadn't greeted me was strange, though, and I half-expected an ambush as Dad pushed through the door. Instead, a bundle of yellow fur jumped up at me.

"Hey, Butterbee." I fell to my knees and fussed her, her wet pink tongue swiping at any section of skin she could find. At least the dog appeared happy to see me— maybe *that* was who Dad meant.

"Two years since you've been here and you greet the

dog first?" Mum hovered over me, hands on her hips. "Bloody typical."

I scrambled to my feet, nearly getting floored by Butterbee in the process. She weaved erratically in the space between us, tail wagging so fast she couldn't walk straight. I brushed at the yellow hairs now covering my black coat, feeling unsure about moving to hug my own mother—which only made things more strange, and me even more unsure. Not even Butterbee's whipping tail could cut through the tension between us.

Mum scowled at my attempt to de-hair myself, but then she took a step forward, her face softening. I knew that look. The "*everything is going to be okay*" look. The one reserved for scraped knees and falling off the neighbour's bike.

"Come here, love."

I rushed into her arms and breathed in her smell. Vanilla and flowery detergent that tickled my nose. *Why had I been so afraid?* I felt eight years old again, rocking in my mother's arms after stubbing my toe on the kitchen cupboard. Emotion swelled in my chest, spilling tears down my face and onto her pink jumper. I couldn't stop them.

What was so disarming about a mother's embrace? The safety, the warmth…the promise that no harm would come to you?

But we all knew that wasn't true. Cameron's death

was enough proof of that.

"Stop being strange and give your daughter a hug, Alan," Mum scolded.

Dad wrapped an arm around me, mumbling something about Mum under his breath. I sighed into the feeling. The bickering and the safety and the…normalness of it all. Except there was one person that wasn't here to greet me. I sobbed into Mum's sleeve, trying to push those thoughts away.

Great start, showing them you're so put together, Holly. You're supposed to be the strong one. I pulled back and wiped my tears with my fingers. I didn't want to set them off too. I couldn't bear to see it.

"Oh, honey." Mum bit her lip, trying to hold back laughter.

"What?" I shrank back, embarrassed about my emotional outburst. I hadn't expected them to start poking fun at it.

Dad's gaze drifted over my face. "You look like one of those emus."

"An emu?"

"He means the emos, love." Mum shook her head, slapping Dad lightly on the arm. "Your mascara is all over your face."

"Oh." I peered into the gold-framed mirror hanging over the fireplace. My eyes were bloodshot and swollen, and black stains were streaked across my eyelids and down my cheeks. An emu might have looked better, to be honest, but at least I didn't smell like one.

Before I could do damage control, the front door opened, the bell declaring someone's arrival. I glanced at my parents. Both were unalarmed that someone had entered their house with such familiarity.

"It's only me!" the voice called, muffled through the wall. Footsteps clunked down the hallway. Butterbee lingered eagerly at the door, waiting to greet her newest playmate. "I've just brought those patterns you wanted."

The door opened, Butterbee pounced, and the owner of the voice revealed herself—the long legs and all the blonde waves of Victoria Castleton.

My heart stumbled, catching itself last minute. She was there. In the flesh. In my parents' living room. Every thought and feeling rushed into my head at the same time, leaving me frozen. *What do I do?*

Victoria giggled, pushing Butterbee down, oblivious or uncaring of my presence as she placed her armful of items on the dining table. A roll of green wool escaped, bouncing along the carpet. Butterbee snatched it in her mouth and made a run for it.

We both reached for the dog at the same time, banging our heads together with a crack. I fell back onto the carpet as a throbbing ache moved through my skull.

My mum fussed over both of us while Dad bribed Butterbee with a cracker to let go of the wool.

I hoped the bang to the head would at least clear my brain, but when our eyes met, the fog remained.

"Holly?" Victoria said, her gaze flicking over me.

"Hello." Hello? Is that the best you've got? "How are you?" So formal. So cringeworthy. Oh, god.

She laughed. A sharp noise, sounding like disbelief. "How am I? How are *you*? It's been…I don't even know how long it's been." Mum helped her to stand, her face lit with joy at experiencing this awkward encounter first-hand. Classic Mum. "I wasn't expecting to see you here…I…" Victoria's blonde eyebrows knotted. "What happened to your face?"

My face? Ah, yes, the "emo emu" look…complete with a pigeon-shit stain on my favourite coat.

Unable to come up with an intelligent answer, or any answer at all to salvage from this humiliating encounter, I scrambled out of the door and up the stairs, careful to avoid the ambush of my dead brother's face. *What an absolutely stellar first impression, Holly. Welcome home.*

The sound of conversation echoed from downstairs, my brain warping it into amusement at my expense. Or perhaps it was, in fact, Cameron, laughing at me from somewhere in a higher plane.

Chapter Four

Once Victoria had gone, I made my way into the living room, face clean but still scarred with embarrassment. Of all the scenarios I'd imagined where we might have reconciled, that was not one of them.

"Well, that was awkward," Dad said, not glancing away from the telly. Butterbee sat in his lap, enjoying the head strokes.

Mum laughed. "Always the observant one, Alan."

I stood awkwardly in front of the Christmas tree, breathing in the smell of pine. Our handmade fingerpainted baubles were still hanging from the branches, sticking out like a sore thumb beside the rest of the gold and red decorations. Cameron and I had made them when we were in primary school. Mum kept everything sentimental like that.

I eyed her suspiciously as she brushed her brown hair behind her ears. "Did you know she was coming?" I asked.

Mum looked at the TV, though I knew for a fact she wasn't interested in the Christmas edition of Dad's favourite car show. "Well, I'd asked Denise for some of her new patterns yesterday—"

"You could've warned me. And since when have you started knitting?"

Her mouth flattened, showing the creases. "It must have slipped my mind with you…coming home, love."

I swallowed. It was my turn to look at the TV. A man with a long beard gushed over a pile of rust disguised as a car. He was wearing a red Christmas hat, but that was about as jolly as it got.

"Sit down then, you're giving me the creeps," Mum said. "Cup of tea?"

I nodded and took a seat on the cream sofa. The upholstery was worn now, displaying several missing chunks in the arms and backs where Butterbee had snacked as puppy.

Dad and I watched the TV in silence while Mum clattered around in the kitchen. The whole street knew when she was making a cup of tea—even Mr Simon could probably hear her a few doors down. My conversation with him replayed, and I cringed. I'd definitely have to pay him a visit at some point; the man was meticulous with his details and had a memory like an elephant. I was going to murder Dani for convincing me this was ever a good idea.

"Hey," Dad said, without looking away from the TV. "Who hides in a bakery?"

"What?"

"Who hides in a bakery?"

I decided to play along. "I don't know. A cosy rat?"

Dad grinned. "A mince spy."

I groaned. "That's terrible."

Mum returned with three steaming mugs, balancing a packet of custard creams under her arm. She eyed my father, who was comfortably reclining in his chair. "Oh, no, don't you hurt yourself, Alan. I'll just struggle, shall I?"

"You were doing such a splendid job, love. I didn't want to take away from your accomplishment."

It hadn't taken long for their bickering to surface. It was like a hobby of theirs. Some people took up tennis doubles or walking; my parents loved to argue. Cameron and I always found it hilarious and used to do impressions of them when they'd gone to bed. Whoever did the best got to play on the PlayStation first.

They'd met at the secondary school here, married at nineteen, and had been inseparable ever since. Their arguing was the binding lifeforce to their way of living;

neither would be able to survive without it.

Mum sat next to me, purposefully moving the biscuits out of Dad's reach. Butterbee twitched her nose in approval, clambering from Dad's lap to mine to get closer to the treats. Mum pursed her lips.

"Just one." She gave Butterbee the corner of a biscuit, and the dog trotted off with her prize into the kitchen.

"Have I mentioned just how radiant you look tonight, sweetheart?" Dad held his hand out, a lopsided smile plastered on his face.

Mum's lips twitched. "A few more times wouldn't hurt."

"Well, you look more stunning every day that I know you."

She shook her head, unable to knock the smile off her face. "You soft sod."

Dad reached for his biscuit, wasting no time before dunking it in his tea.

"Really, Dad, all that for a biscuit?"

"Not just any biscuit, Hol, these are the M&S ones. Top quality."

Mum offered me one, and I declined. "Didn't you hear the man?" she said. "They're from M&S."

"I'm fine, thanks." I wasn't sure my stomach could handle anything right now. Spewing up on Mum's red rug would be the cherry on the cake for this fantastic disaster of a "welcome home".

"More for me, then," Dad commented, reaching for another.

Mum smacked his hand away. "Maybe you should start taking note. You're getting rounder by the day."

"Leave me alone, Trace, it's your daughter you should be interrogating, not me." Dad flashed me a smile before returning his attention to the TV.

Mum considered this, swivelling around so she could question me more thoroughly. She brushed her dark hair back, letting it fall around her face. "Where do we start?"

I sipped my tea, but it was still too hot. The bearded man on the screen broke something off under the bonnet, chuckling like Santa Claus. I pretended to be interested in his words.

"Holly. What's going on with Vicky?"

The horror of our first encounter after two years flashed into my brain. I wanted to drown in my cup of tea.

"Nothing, Mum. We haven't spoken since…"

"Since Cameron died?"

Her words jolted through my spine. "Mum, please."

"It's been two years, Holly."

The waves of grief swirled in my chest. "I don't want to talk about it."

Her thin brows drew together in frustration. "You can't just pretend it never happened, Hol. We need—"

Flashbacks assaulted me, a shard of pain stabbing

into my heart. "Mum, no!" Without realising it, I'd already stood to leave. My flight or fight instinct had kicked in, surging through my veins and screaming at me to run.

Mum watched me carefully, like someone approaching a stray dog. Her expression softened. "Okay, love. Not tonight." She patted the seat next to her. "What about Vicky?"

I sighed, letting my squeezed fists relax and drop to my sides. Fine.

How could I explain my relationship with Vicky? Things with us had never been simple, even before Cameron's death. Now it just seemed utterly hopeless. What could you say to someone to make up for one of your biggest regrets? Nothing could change the past.

Memories involuntarily unpacked themselves, things that I'd tried to keep locked away in the recesses of my mind. Like that summer night in Vicky's bedroom when she'd first kissed me. How everything inside had spun and the puzzle pieces finally made sense. How terrified that made me. The fear of being different. How that had pushed me into the arms of Cameron's friend Billy, and how it had crushed Vicky's heart. I regretted it every day.

"Things are just different now, Mum."

She offered me back the tea I'd offloaded to her and sipped her own, her eyes cast to the side in the way she does whenever she's thinking. "Things *are* different, love.

And I know life will never be the same. But…it doesn't mean that all is lost."

My hands tightened around the mug. Not only did Vicky remind me so much of Cameron, but I'd messed up—more than a few times. And without Cameron's help, we might never have got past it. He always knew the right thing to say, and he never judged my decisions, even when I acted like a coward.

It had taken time, and involved some awkward moments, but Vicky and I had stayed friends throughout our studies and my move to London. Our friendship was more than just those underlying scary feelings for each other. We moved past it, but there was always that rainbow elephant in the room. Those moments where we had both been caught in the crosshair, but neither of us had wanted to talk about it.

Then I'd ditched her again when Cameron died, crawling into my own personal hell of grief. How were we supposed to talk about that? And how could we ever do that now, without Cameron mediating?

Not the best thing you've ever done, Holly.

I wanted to bang my head against the mantelpiece until all the Christmas cards fell off.

"I know she's missed you, Hol." Mum's gaze burned into my face, but I couldn't look at her. "Why don't you pop round tomorrow and say hello?"

Nausea wrestled with my insides. Heat rippled up my

neck.

"I've missed her too, Mum," I said quietly, barely audible over Butterbee's snores, who'd returned from snaffling her biscuit and now snoozed on the rug.

"Big journeys begin with small steps," Dad said, eyes fixed on the TV.

Mum and I turned to look at him, dumbfounded. Since when did my dad start spouting wisdom like Nelson Mandela?

Mum smiled. "That's beautiful, Alan."

"It's graffitied on the side of the Co-op."

The smile dropped from her face. "Oh, right." She shook her head, then placed her hand on my knee. "He's right though, love. Small steps. You've just got to take the first one."

Chapter Five

The morning chill of the countryside frosted the grass, each blade sparkling in the early light. I pushed the blue chequered curtains wider, heaving in a deep sigh. *A new day…in my old house. Weird.*

My room was a time capsule of a younger me. A stark contrast to my sleek and modern—slightly on the smaller side—apartment in London. Faded blue walls matched the chequered curtains and bedding, bathing the room in a hue of muted sadness. Pictures of me, Cameron, and Vicky lined the wooden dresser, the odd abandoned bottles of make-up still rattling around the drawers. Clumpy foundation and sticky cheap eyeliner. The type of stuff I wouldn't be seen dead wearing today.

The white wardrobe was empty, bar my red poufy

prom dress—another night I'd not care to remember. As the wardrobe door clunked shut, my bedroom door opened.

"I thought I heard noises." Mum raised her eyebrows. "You're up early."

"Not really. I'm always up early for work."

She bobbed her head. "Ah, yes. Advertising."

"That's the one." Despite years of painfully explaining what it is I actually do for a living, believe it or not, this was actually progress.

"Anyway," Mum went on, "I'm going to nip to the stables. Wondered if you wanted to join?" Her dark eyes sparkled with hope. Hope far misplaced. I could think of fifty things I'd rather do than shift horse shit into a wheelbarrow.

"Maybe tomorrow."

I didn't miss how her shoulders dipped. "Alright, love. Cup of tea? I'll put the kettle on." She ducked out of the door.

I collapsed on the old swivel chair and looked about the room. More memories surfaced. Cameron reading our school reports out like a news announcer, standing on the chair while I tried to spin him off it. The two of us, jumping on the bed, trying out a new wrestling move we'd seen on TV—both ending up somersaulting and crashing headfirst into the dresser. I felt over the scar on my elbow thoughtfully, remembering the horror on Mum's face when she saw all the blood.

"I'll see you later, Hol. Cuppa is on the counter!" The door shook as Mum closed it, and she strode down the drive, wrapped up in a purple scarf and an ugly orange hat with tassels. The little blue Fiat looked ridiculous next to my BMW—or rather, my BMW looked ridiculous next to the Fiat. A wave of imposter syndrome covered me again, and suddenly I felt like a stranger in my own house.

Movement through the window, followed by a muffled shout, distracted me enough to stop me descending into a whirl of self-doubt. Vicky emerged from the house next door, tight-fitting black trousers sculpting her legs, a cute woolly hat pulled over her blonde head. She waved to my mum, who was still trying to reverse off the drive, and got in her own car. *Where is she going?* A stone sunk into my stomach with the realisation I had no idea about her life now.

I watched them both leave through the window, living out my best stalker-neighbour fantasy, and then remembered my tea downstairs.

With Dad at work, Butterbee and I snuggled up on the sofa watching daytime TV. The run-up to Christmas had the presenters showcasing "Christmas hacks" that looked both cheap and terrible. They tried to pass them off to the cameras, but their fake smiles and over-coiffed hair wouldn't work on even the most gullible frugalist. Unless your goal was to piss off each family member with a homemade turd of a present, or possibly poison them with a homemade Christmas pudding that looked like it'd come out the rear end of a reindeer. Already the free space in my day irritated me; I hated not having things to do. The loneliness would creep in and open my mind up to wallowing—very dangerous indeed.

Mum returned sometime later, red-faced, hair stuck up in opposite directions.

"What are you doing?" she asked.

I hovered, yellow duster in hand. "I, er, reorganised the DVDs. And your bookshelf."

A smile played on her mouth. "I can see that. I was just wondering…why?" Unable to contain it, she burst into laughter.

"Well, I…I don't know, to be honest." I giggled. Mum's laughter was contagious and unmistakably owl-like. She hooted and cooed until she couldn't take any more, and then unwound the purple scarf from her neck, drooping it over the dining chair.

"Holly, if I didn't know better, I'd say you were procrastinating."

"I didn't have anything to do."

She raised her eyebrows, and the smile dropped from her face. "I'd say quite the opposite. Small steps…Mending bridges? Ring any bells?"

It was difficult to explain why I hadn't ventured next door yet without mentioning how I'd been spying through the window. Even harder to explain—and I cannot stress this enough—how the thought of seeing Vicky again after our last encounter made me want to swim all the two hundred miles downriver to the safety of the Thames. And I hated swimming.

I sighed, slowly pushing the cloth over the wooden sideboard.

"I didn't realise how bad this was eating you up, love. I mean, it must be, if you're cleaning."

We both laughed again. Butterbee scampered over, trying to pinch the cloth from my hands. After a half-hearted game of tug-o-war, she relented, slumping down on the rug in defeat.

I knew the feeling. "How do I even know she wants to see me, Mum? I've been a bit of a shit, really."

Mum's gaze softened. "You'll just have to trust me on this one."

Feeling out of place left a strange taste in my mouth. I wasn't sure; everything felt off.

"Do you want me to come with you?" she asked.

"Oh, no. That'd be pathetic."

"More pathetic than hiding in here and cleaning your mother's DVD collection?"

I hid my face in my hands. "Oh, god, you're right. I am pathetic."

She placed a soft hand on my shoulder. "Get dressed. Get a grip. And get going."

"Very motivational, Mum," I mumbled. "You should write a book."

She seemed to consider this for a moment before waving the idea away with her hand. "Rubbish. I'm far too busy for that."

I suppressed a snort. The idea that my mum considered working one day a week at the Post Office "too busy" always tickled me.

"Go on, then." She shooed me towards the door. "If it goes badly, you can always dust the kitchen cupboards. They need organising too, actually…"

I took my cue to leave and left Mum muttering to herself in the living room. Avoiding the pictures in the hallway, on the stairs, and in my bedroom, I dressed in pale blue jeans and a thick white jumper. I didn't want to look like I'd spent too much time trying to look presentable, even if it took longer than I cared to admit. But I did need to do some damage control after the emo, shit-stain look of last night.

Before I could talk myself out of it, I walked the twenty steps from my house to the Castletons' and knocked on the door. *Please be out. Please be out. Please be out.* If I hadn't been so preoccupied with the way I'd dressed, I might've noticed Vicky's car parked back on the kerb. If I had, I might have had something prepared to say to her.

Instead, the door opened, and my brain refused to function when those questioning blue eyes fell on mine.

Chapter Six

Since moving to London, I'd never been lonely. Talking to women was one of the few things I would say I was good at. There was always a bar or a club, the friend of a friend, or someone waiting on the other end of a swipe right, like my ex Katie.

It's a fair estimation that I was off my game here. Facing my family after a two-year hiatus, seeing my brother's ghost in every corner of the house, and running into Vicky Castleton were all contributing to this embarrassing showdown of wordlessness on the Castletons' front step.

I sucked a deep breath in, pushed out my chest with false confidence, and forced a smile. "Hey, Victoria."

Her eyebrows bounced slightly, amusement playing

on her features. "Since when have you called me Victoria? Only my great-aunt Pat called me that."

All false confidence dwindled away. "Yeah, I remember her. How is she?"

"She died in April. Dad found her at the bottom of her stairs."

Fuck. I crossed my arms, the cold nipping through my jumper. "Oh, god. I'm sorry. That's terrible."

"She was old. They think she had a heart attack."

"I'm sorry. She…seemed nice."

The left corner of her mouth tugged upwards, showing her dimple. "Yeah, she was. I could read you her obituary if you'd like, but I don't think that's why you're really here."

I laughed awkwardly. "No, actually, I just wanted to say hello. Properly. Last night, I…er, well…"

Vicky let me squirm a little more before moving aside to invite me in. The warmth of the house was instantly comforting, along with the familiar smell I associated so much with my teenage years.

I pushed aside thoughts of Cameron as Vicky led me to the kitchen. She filled the kettle and fetched two mugs from the cupboard before leaning back on the counter.

Her gaze roamed over me, assessing, before she met my eyes. There was a newfound confidence there, almost like the two of us had traded places from all those years ago. Any hint of shyness had long washed away, creeping its way into me instead. Vicky was beautiful—that was no question—but speaking to her shouldn't be so difficult. What was happening to me?

She brushed a hand through her blonde hair, the curls bouncing back to frame her face. The kettle hummed in the background, filling the air with anticipation. I took a seat at the wooden island and met Vicky's stare.

"I'm sorry about yesterday," I said. "I didn't have the best day and, well, I was very surprised to see you."

"Did you forget I lived next door?" she asked playfully.

"No, but the last time Mum mentioned you, she said you'd moved, so I wasn't sure."

The kettle clicked, steam fanning into the air.

"Well, I did, but I'm back again. For now." Did that mean a recent break-up? Vicky poured the cups, her back to me. I couldn't help but admire the shape of her legs in the dark denim. She must really enjoy the gym. She glanced over her shoulder, and I snapped my eyes up. "You still take sugar?"

I nodded, a little shocked that she remembered. *I hope she didn't see me checking her out.*

She stirred and handed the mug to me with a smile. "Are you still down south?"

"Yeah. I'm on the advertising team for Pertoni Clark."

Her eyes widened. "Is that the guy that invented the

self-sweeping broom?"

"That's the one."

"The one that gets itself stuck and some started catching fire?"

I grimaced. "Yep. But that's all been sorted out now. Just a little product malfunction."

"Well, that's very cool." Vicky smiled, genuinely meaning it. I relaxed a little. "I'm just finishing my master's in business, actually," she went on.

"That's awesome. Would you ever want to start your own?"

Vicky took a sip from her mug. "Maybe someday. I need to find somewhere for some practical experience first."

The wheels in my head turned. "I could always talk to my boss and see if they could help you out?"

Her face lit up. "That would be really great, Hol. Thank you."

I smiled back, happy to elicit that response from her. "No problem. It's based in London though, so I'm not sure how that would work."

She drummed her fingers on the table thoughtfully, but I didn't miss the smile slipping from her face. "I'm not sure I'd like living in the city. But…never say never, I guess."

I hated how excited that made me feel. The smallest seed of hope planted itself in my stomach, and immediately I tried to smother it. I didn't need any of those feelings resurfacing. "Really?"

"I'm not sure. I just can't picture myself there. But then again, I can't picture you there either, and you seem to be doing well."

I sipped my tea. I was unsure how to respond when people said I was doing well. What did that even mean, really? I was functioning, sure. But well? That seemed a stretch.

"So how long are you here for?" she asked.

"Just until Boxing Day."

The conversation lulled when we both took another drink from our mugs. The sweetness really hit a spot; I was delighted to see Vicky still made a great cup of tea.

Despite her gaze on me, I relaxed into my seat. With the hard beginning part and the awkward conversation about Vicky's great-aunt Pat out of the way, my mojo started to awaken. I was Holly Bradfield; I could talk to Vicky. We'd been best friends for years.

"So—" I started.

"How—"

I grinned. "Go on, you go first."

She leaned forward, and I caught a whiff of her flowery perfume. Her mouth slackened, and I suddenly feared what was going to come out of it.

"How are you doing about Cameron?"

Just like that, the sickness was back. The itchy,

helpless feeling in my limbs. *Why couldn't people just let things be?* I wanted to be better…to be Holly again. I couldn't do that when faced with the loss of Cameron every five minutes.

I looked down into my tea, unable to stand the pity in her eyes. "I'm fine."

"I'm serious, Holly. I want to know how you are. After you basically dropped off the face of the earth—"

A loud and repulsive ringtone cut Vicky off mid-sentence, and she fished her phone out of her pocket. She scowled slightly at the name.

"Sorry," she said. "I just need to get this."

"Sure." I let out a breath, thankful that the distraction gods were on my side for a change. They tended to mock me with phone calls that interrupted a woman's leaning-in kiss or quick clothing removal. One time, a bird flew into the windshield as a woman and I were driving back to her place. She was so distraught about having hurt it, she ended up asking me to leave before I'd even stepped foot inside her apartment. Bet it was one of those pesky pigeons.

The distraction on Vicky's end didn't seem like a good one. The conversation on the phone got heated, though she was trying to stay hushed for my sake. Annoyingly, I couldn't catch much. I wanted to collect all the pieces so I could build a picture of her life now. It was a strange feeling, being caught in the middle. So much had changed, but so much was the same. Like the warm feeling growing in her presence.

When she hung up, a red tinge coated her cheeks. She sat in the seat next to me, shaking her head.

"Everything okay?" I asked.

She sighed, blowing into her mug. "Tanya was supposed to help me out tonight at the village fair, but she's cancelled last minute. Some late-notice modelling drop-out or something."

I nodded, like the name Tanya meant anything to me. "What are you doing at the village fair?"

"Mum has a stall space selling her handmade stuff there—knitted scarfs, bags and such—but she can't run it because she's working tonight." She tucked some blonde strands behind her ear, revealing three little hoop earrings. Cute. "I said I'd help out, but it's a lot of work for one person."

"I'm not busy tonight if you need a hand." The words were out of my mouth before I'd had a chance to think about them.

She grinned. "You'd be a lifesaver! Are you sure?"

I smiled back, feeling my pulse quicken. *Has she always looked so cute when she smiles?* "Of course. I'd be happy to. What time do you need me?"

"It starts at seven, but I need to be there at least two hours before to set everything up."

"I'll pick you up, then. Four-thirty?"

She laughed, the movement reaching her eyes. "I mean, it's quite the drive. Are you sure you can manage it in that fancy car?"

Ah, so she's clocked my BMW then. "If it gives me an excuse to spend time with you, then I'm sure I'll manage."

Vicky failed to suppress the surprise as it flickered across her face. *Where did that come from? Careful, Holly. Don't fall into bad habits.*

I stumbled over myself, trying to rescue my comment. "I mean, uh, we've got a lot to catch up on. It's been a while. And I'd like that." I drained the last of my tea—hoping the mug would shield the red spreading to my cheeks—thanked her, and then headed for the door. Clearly I needed to pull myself together before tonight if I intended to make any impression on Vicky Castleton.

I almost stumbled on the step.

Since when was that my goal? Did I even want to impress her? Her smile flashed in my mind, stirring something long forgotten in the pit of my stomach.

Yes, actually, I think I do.

Chapter Seven

As I deposited the fifth box of sellable items into the boot of my car, I regretted wearing heels. I chastised myself, debating whether I should change into my comfortable trainers back home and face the music of Mum's *I told you so.* Channelling and misplacing the "small steps" mantra, I nearly twisted my ankle twice trying to make the journey across the cobbled driveway. Vicky denied it, but I swear she laughed.

Once piled up to the brim, disrupting the cleanliness of my BMW and the sight of my rearview mirror, we drove the short distance to the village hall. A gravelled path led us around the back of the old stone building. Memories of school choir days, village harvest festivals, and fairs played through my mind. Cameron and I had always complained about those types of events; we'd much rather stay at home and play. Mum would lure us in with the promise of a shared bag of pick 'n' mix, which always ended in a fight over the last gummy worm.

In the winter darkness, the hall seemed much smaller than I remembered. It acted as the village's hub for many things, including church on Sundays, ceremonies for the local school, and basically anything the locals hoped would raise a bit of money and keep the community going. Ivy crawled up the walls to the tall gable roof, lit up by the Three Wise Men flashing on the front of the building.

White marquees promised tasty food around the side of the hall, with freshly baked mince pies and Christmas doughnuts showing Santa's big jolly face. Generators hummed away as people dashed about their tasks, decorating colourful chalkboards and setting cutlery in neat stacks for future customers.

The combination of furniture polish and the smell of musty attic assaulted my nose as we entered through the old wooden doors of the hall. Familiar faces were already busying themselves, decorating their tables with arts and crafts, and pictures and paintings of the local area.

Vicky directed us to her empty table, and I cursed Jimmy Choo for the torture devices attached to my feet. Manual labour wasn't my thing, but it still surprised me just how heavy some of the boxes were as we trailed back and forth to bring them all inside. The last bag at the back of the boot looked squished and a little torn, so I opened it up to check the damage. Instead of scarves and stuffed animals, a familiar hoodie looked back at me.

It was Katie's. Ugh. I'd forgotten about the bag of her belongings I'd removed from my apartment. I'd been meaning to drop it off at hers when she wasn't in, but it'd slipped my mind. I pushed it to the back of the boot and closed it. I didn't want Vicky to see it and get the wrong idea. I'd deal with it later.

The doors to the fair opened an hour afterwards, and a steady stream of locals entered, eager to browse the village's junk. I eyed a gentleman manning a stall on the other side of the hall. His aged whiskeys and liquors looked more appetising by the minute. Stupid damn feet. The cold didn't help either.

"Are you sure you're okay?" Vicky asked, jarring me from my daydream of necking a bottle of vodka. "You seem like you're in pain."

"I'm fine. Just a little sore." *Emotionally and mentally too.* I forced a smile, but Vicky didn't seem convinced.

"I did say you should've changed your shoes. Maybe I wasn't clear that the job required some lifting." She turned to greet a customer before casting another sympathetic look my way.

What a way to come across as incompetent, Holly.

Wearing heels in London gave off a certain status. Women admired that sacrifice: feet for power. Strutting around at a head height over your peers hinted at dominance. Confidence. Sex. Of course, I'd never worn heels in winter while moving thirty boxes down a wonky driveway and into a hall before. Lesson learned.

Instead of impressing Vicky after the shitshow that was our first encounter, I'd just made myself seem more ignorant. *Just grin and bear it.*

We served a few customers, selling handmade bookmarks and embroidered journals, even some cute little knitted farm animals. An old lady bought several knitted jumpers, gushing about how she was going to gift them to her grandchildren.

Vicky and I shared a look after she'd left, waiting until she'd pottered to the baked goods table to fawn over a scone.

"I mean, I love my mum's work," Vicky started. "I really do. I wouldn't have convinced her to do this kind of thing if I didn't. But...those poor grandkids. An 'I heart Mistleberry' jumper?"

We burst out laughing as another customer walked up to our stall, browsing some woollen hats.

"There's some lovely things here, ain't that right, Margaret?" The man turned to his wife, who was busy stuffing toffees into her mouth. He shook his head and smiled at us. "Some crackin' work here, girls. Wonderful to see it."

I held up my hands. "I can't take any credit. It's all the Castletons' talent."

Vicky glanced at me, a smile pulling at her mouth. "Well, my mum mostly, yes."

He bought a blue-and-white hat and moved along, tugging Margaret behind him.

"So, your mum made most of this?" I said, admiring an adorable knitted Rudolph keychain. "Have you made any?"

"Well…I did make a few things. Like, erm…this!" Vicky held up a cross-stitch tote bag. A rather sad-looking cow posed on the front, its right leg longer than its left.

I'd seen the monstrosity earlier but had swallowed my comment, thinking Denise must've intended some deep meaning behind it. Seeing its lopsided head again, I couldn't believe she'd allowed Vicky to sell it.

"Wow… What's wrong with its face?"

Vicky's nose twitched, and she looked up at me. "What do you mean? Don't you think it's cute?"

I baulked at her, eyeing the squished nose and the questionable stitchwork. "Cute isn't what springs to mind. It's the stuff of nightmares: killer cow murders family while sleeping."

"You're terrible!" Vicky's made to swat me with the bag, but I managed to dodge out of her way. Our eyes locked, and her smile warmed something inside my chest.

Slowly, her face fell serious. "Holly, there is something that I wanted to talk to you about too." She dropped her gaze to her hands.

Oh, no. Does she want to bring up our past now? Right here?

A flustered woman holding a child by each hand clattered up to the stall. "Kevin, no! Kyle, put that back!" The poor woman's limbs were pulled left and right, like a marionette on a string. One of the young boys, chocolate smeared around his face, started prodding his sticky fingers at the animal hats.

"I'll be right back." Vicky jumped up to assist the woman trying to prise a crocheted turtle from her son's pudgy hand.

I blew out a breath. We'd been having such a good time, I didn't want to darken it with any serious discussions. I hadn't stopped smiling all night; it felt just like old times. Easy. Fun. We always seemed to slip back into our relationship quickly—that was one of the great things about us. *Still great at avoiding things too.* I pushed the voices in my head away. Why did they always have to sound like my mother?

After one of the evening's more entertaining sales— the poor woman ended up forking out for two chocolate- smeared knitted Father Christmases and a torn-in-half bookmark—the hall started to wind down a little.

Stalls had cleared of their stock, leaving happy faces

counting their pennies behind empty tables. As a couple left through the doors, the aroma of roast meat and spiced potatoes drifted in.

"You hungry?" Vicky asked. "I could eat a horse."

"Not a cow?" I nodded towards the ghastly tote bag.

Vicky shook her head. "It's a work of art," she told me. "You unartistic folk wouldn't understand true genius." She flicked her hair over her shoulder before turning serious. "Do you want some food or not? Don't mess with me. Hell hath no fury like a woman starved."

I held up my palms in mock surrender. "I remember what happens when you're hungry. Some food sounds great."

"Wise choice. You comfortable watching the stall?"

"Sure." I reached into my bag and pulled out my purse. "Here, I'll get it."

"It's fine. I'm sure I can manage ten quid."

"No, no, here. Any of those are fine."

"Very fancy-pants." She raised her eyebrows, eying the multitude of cards in my hand. "And so stubborn. Nice to see that hasn't changed, at least." She studied me for a moment. Then a smile stretched across her face as she plucked one of the cards from my grip. "Alright, you rest your feet then, princess. I'll be back before you can say 'pillow'."

I watched her leave with an open mouth, surprised that my offer to pay seemed to have backfired. Should I have gone to get the food instead? If I'd suggested that, she'd probably have reacted in the same way. But that was Vicky Castleton: unexpected. Always unexpected. One day she's your best friend, the next she's kissing you in her bedroom.

But a pillow princess? Pfft. She knew that comment would irk me.

Had I changed? I considered her other remark and guessed she was right. Lots of things had changed. Just two weeks ago, I was with Katie at her parents' house in Devon, trying to pretend everything was fine, and now...

I was sitting in my hometown's old village hall, staring at the perky, round bum of my first kiss as she disappeared through the doors.

Huh, life is weird.

Vicky returned with two plates of steaming hot dogs. From the size of her smirk, you might think she'd just found twenty quid blowing around outside. Freshly cooked, perfectly salted meat, with cranberry sauce and a generous helping of crispy potato fritters piled high on the plate.

It was a masterpiece. Truly.

"That looks fucking amazing," I said, practically dribbling.

"I know right?" She handed me my plate, and we dug in, wasting no time contemplating our surroundings or thinking about how much we resembled Denise's knitted pigs sitting in front of us.

Finally, with bloated bellies, we sat back in our chairs, watching the last of the people browsing the stalls. I wanted to bring up Vicky's comments again, but I didn't know how.

My vision caught on a balding man examining a fruitcake across the hall. "Oh, my god. Is that Mr Wickham?"

Vicky leaned closer, her sweet perfume intoxicating my senses. "Oh, god, it is! Remember when he used to make you stand outside in science class?"

Vicky's face was so close to mine that I could count her freckles. If she just turned her head, and I turned mine, our lips would be inches apart. *I wonder if she still kisses the same…*

When I didn't answer, she leaned back, side-eying me. "Don't you remember?"

Our kiss? I swallowed. "I do, yeah." *Oh, right, Mr Wickham.* "He hated us sitting next to each other. What was that he used to call us? The Jabber…somethings?"

"The Jabberwockies!"

"That's it!" I laughed, and Vicky joined in.

We recalled more memories from school: sneaking out of P.E. to watch YouTube videos in the toilets; Vicky starring as Friar Tuck in the school play; all the time we used to spend lying back on the grass, picking animals out of the clouds.

When our laughter subsided, my belly ached. I couldn't remember the last time I'd been so full, or had smiled so much. Not since Cameron died, anyway.

Vicky and I had always been that way—except for after prom night. I hoped she didn't think about that day as much as I did. The way her face had crumpled when I told her I'd be going with Billy instead of her still haunted my dreams. But I was scared back then. I wasn't ready to announce myself to the world. It didn't mean my feelings disappeared.

There'd always been a question mark above Vicky's head. Throughout the years, we'd come close but had never crossed that line again. Not since the night in her bedroom.

Vicky's hand playfully brushed my knee, and my breath hitched. "Thanks for helping me out tonight," she said. "It would have been a lot more shit if you weren't here."

"That's an unusual thank you."

She grinned, and my eyes were drawn to her mouth. "I can't be giving you too many compliments," she said. "Don't want you getting an even bigger head."

"Excuse me? An *even* bigger head?"

She chuckled, shaking her head. "Yeah. You're...you're different."

My gaze drifted over her face. "Well, you're different too. But in a good way."

Her eyes flickered to mine, and she pursed her lips, eyebrows rising slightly. Then, with the flick of a switch, she jumped to her feet, her expression wiped clean of any deep thought. "Come on, then, let's get this stuff back in your Rolls Royce, shall we?"

"It's not that fancy," I muttered and stood, easing onto my aching feet. "Right," I said, "let's go—"

The floor fell from under me with a sharp snap, my chin connecting with the edge of the table. My tongue caught between my teeth like a vice, muffling my attempt at a scream.

Pain seared through me as I fell to the dusty floor, cursing Mr Choo for all the inconvenience he'd caused tonight. These shoes should come with a warning: s*hit for anything requiring physical effort. Prone to collapse in front of attractive women.*

A crowd of mildly concerned shoppers gathered around. *This is so embarrassing.*

Vicky offered me a hand, and I took it. Heat sizzled from the touch of her skin. "Come on, princess. Let's get you home."

My feet throbbed and my face ached, but my pride was the most bruised as she helped me up.

"I'm not a princess," I grumbled, rubbing my throbbing lip.

Vicky's laughter echoed through the hall, making it impossible not to smile. *Ouch.*

Despite the aches and pains, and the no doubt relentless teasing I'd receive for this, it'd been one of the best days I'd had in a long time. But did Vicky feel the same spark I did?

Her eyes met mine, and I swear something inside me clicked.

I had six days left to find out.

Chapter Eight

Dani's cackle ripped through the speaker, and I pulled my phone from my ear. "You mean you were covered in actual bird shit when you ran into Vicky?"

"I wiped it off. I didn't just leave it on there, Dani. I wasn't saving it for later."

"That serves you right for keeping this piece of juicy gossip from me."

"I didn't keep anything from you. It just kinda slipped my mind." I looked up at the white ceiling, tracing a pattern with my finger. Lying on my bed like this used to be my thinking place. I'd hoped taking some time could help me make some sense of my feelings for Vicky, but my best friend had other ideas.

"Did you at least take a picture?"

"Of Vicky? No, I'm not a creep."

"No, of you...covered in shit." She laughed again, on the verge of losing control and progressing into the laughing wail associated with Dani's level-three funniness. "We could make it the banner picture at work for a month. Mr Clark would love that, surely."

"No, surprisingly, I didn't take a picture. Can you focus, please?"

"I'm sorry. I'm sorry." There was a muffled sound on her end as she took a deep breath in. "I'm good now. So, this Vicky girl was your first kiss? The girl in her bedroom?"

"Yes."

"I can't believe you didn't tell me she might be at your parents'! What's your plan?"

"Well, I didn't think she would be." I sighed, pushing my head back into the pillow. Truth be told, whenever Vicky popped into my head, I'd pushed it away—until now. Like Cameron, I tended to squash those feelings down. It was safer that way. But there were many nights from my teenage years where I'd lie in this exact spot, thinking about Vicky, about what kissing a girl meant. Wondering if dating Billy would "set me straight".

I was confident in my sexuality now, but sometimes, if I scrunched my eyes hard enough, it was almost as if the last ten years hadn't happened. I'd trace the ceiling with my fingers and daydream about Vicky, trying to interpret her actions and the things she said. Cameron would play his music too loud, and I'd stomp next door. Instead of telling him off, he'd show me the latest video for the music he was listening to, and we'd just end up doing something silly together. He always had a talent for disarming me. Even when I didn't want him to.

Now that room was a hotbed of emotional torment. I couldn't even bear to look at the door when I passed it in the hallway.

With a blink, the fabric of reality rearranged itself. Strands of those times still threaded themselves into the present, but the present was tainted now. Never again would Cameron call me from his room, or burst into mine with a smile on his face. Those strands still wove themselves into my heart, but where they used to leave a warm comfort, they now only left a deep ache.

"Holly? Do you have a plan of action?"

The strands snapped, and the cold slap of truth hit me. Cameron was dead. He always would be. Nothing could bring him back or thaw the ice in my chest.

I brushed away the tears on my cheeks. "A plan? No, I don't know what to do."

"Well, do you still feel the same?" she asked. "Is there a spark there between you?"

Vicky's smile replayed in my mind. The soft dimple in her left cheek, and the way her eyes lit up. Hot, gooey honey swirled in my stomach. A feeling that I knew well.

But it slowly dwindled away like water down the drain, replaced with thoughts of Cameron.

"I think there is, yeah. But it's complicated." I swallowed. "Cameron...you know, the three of us were really close. She reminds me so much of him and..."

Tears threatened again. I covered my mouth with my hand to stifle the sobs. Once these floodgates opened, they'd drown me. I couldn't let that happen again.

Dani was quiet for a minute. Her steady breathing on the end of the line was a comfort. A lifeline to cling onto with both hands. After a few minutes, my own breathing slowed.

"If you think there's something there, Holly, don't run from it. You can't keep running from the past forever."

"I know that, I do, but it's not just that. I...I shut her out after Cameron died. I don't really know why she's even talking to me."

"Don't be so hard on yourself. Grief is hard. But maybe...maybe an apology wouldn't be the worst place to start."

I looked at my nails. The paint had chipped from moving all the boxes yesterday. Reconnecting with her had been better even than I remembered. Vicky's laugh entered my mind, the way her nose crinkled in the cutest way. *Damn it.* I sighed. "Yeah. Maybe you're right."

"As if there should be any doubt."

"Thanks, Dani. I owe you one."

"You owe me nothing. Love you!"

"Love you too."

With Dani's comforting voice gone, the loneliness started to creep back in. I lay still for a while, letting my thoughts untangle themselves. *Can I see a future with Vicky? Do I even want that?*

Time had been good to her, and if I were honest with myself, I'd thought about her more often than I cared to admit. I'd wanted to reach out and bridge the gap, but pride had got in the way. My mind had always convinced me that she'd be better off without me, that she'd moved on, that she didn't even remember. But when things got quiet and my thoughts settled, they always found Vicky.

There was a sharp rap on the door, and Mum poked her head in. "Fancy helping me with the horses?" Her brows furrowed, and she hurried to the bed. "What's wrong, love? Have you been crying?"

I waved her away. "Oh, no, no. I'm fine."

"Holly, please. Talk to me. I'm your mother; I did give birth to you. I know when there's something wrong."

I knew her fuss stemmed from a good place, but the attention poked at the raw places in my chest. The last thing I wanted was to cry in front of her again. She needed to know I was okay. I didn't want to put my problems on her. She deserved better.

"I'm just a bit tired, that's all."

She scooted closer, bouncing the mattress, and moved her hand to my knee, patting it softly. "We can talk about him, Holly. It's a good thing. To remember him."

"Mum," I said softly. "Please stop."

"Is it something to do with Vicky?" she asked, her tone rising an octave.

I sat up so I could observe her closer. "What about Vicky?"

She removed her hand and tugged down her burgundy gilet. "Well, you know, we always suspected a little something going on between the two of you and…"

"Mum," I warned. "What did you do?"

"Nothing, nothing," she flustered, unable to meet my gaze.

Something clicked in my mind. "Did you mean for Vicky to come round here with the wool the other night? To get us speaking again?"

A coat of red flushed her cheeks. "I was just giving you a little push, that's all, love."

"Mum," I groaned, feeling like a stroppy teenager. "That's so uncool."

"Well, at the rate you're going, your father and I would just be stars in the sky. And I do want some grandchildren before I die."

I covered my face with my hands and groaned again, louder.

"What? I do! Your dad says Butterbee is enough, but

I need a chubby grandchild to feed chocolate to."

I guess I am her last hope now. I peeked through my fingers. Mum's face glowed in some far-off dream of imaginary grandchildren. Talking about children seemed a bit premature, though, when I couldn't even muster the courage to talk to Vicky about our past.

Mum turned back to me. "So, fancy coming to help with the horses?"

"Maybe tomorrow."

"You said that yesterday," she grumbled, crossing her arms. "Come on, love. It'll be like when you were a little kid. You haven't been to see them in years."

Cameron and I spent many mornings and evenings "helping" Mum with the horses. I still admired them— they were much smarter than many people thought—but I didn't have the dedication Mum did. The horse bug, as Dad called it. Mum wanted me to follow in her footsteps, but I just had too much fear. There was something about the horses I couldn't quite trust. Cameron and I used to spend most of the time playing hide-and-seek in the stables instead.

"I think I know of a way to persuade you." Mum smiled at me knowingly. "I have my suspicions that a certain blonde you may or may not like will be there."

Vicky? "What? Why?"

She smirked at my sudden change in posture. "She has a mare in the stables too."

She does? "Why didn't you tell me?"

"Well, because, love, and I mean this in the nicest way"—Mum patted my knee—"not everything revolves around you." She cracked into laughter, but her words had a bite of truth to them. Standing, she brushed down her gilet and picked a few yellow Butterbee hairs from her trousers. "Come on now, get dressed. Let's go get me some grandchildren."

Chapter Nine

A cold, biting wind greeted me as soon as I stepped out of Mum's Fiat. The land where Mum rented her stable sat at the very top of a hill, making it extra exposed to the elements.

I followed Mum down the gravel track a little sheepishly, trying to keep my hat attached to my head and avoid any stray piles of horse poo. I spotted Biscuit, Mum's beautiful ginger gelding, on the other side of the big open field, stretching his large head through the fence to reach the longer grass.

A wheelbarrow indicated someone inside one of the four stables. Mum turned to me and said something, but her words got carried away by the wind.

I gritted my teeth as we approached. Mum had

promised not to mention anything relating to children or grandchildren, but the woman could be a wild card. Inside the stable, Vicky was working away absentmindedly, tidying up the sawdust bedding with a pitchfork. I'd be lying if I said the sight of her lost in her own world didn't squeeze my insides. *Who knew that a messy ponytail and tattered jodhpurs could look so good?*

"Look who I've finally persuaded to come," Mum announced, leaning in the stable door.

Vicky jumped, flinging shavings everywhere. "God, Tracy, you scared the life outta me!" Her blue eyes found mine. Seeing her smile made the strong stench of piss and shit worth it. "Well, well, look what we have here," she said. "A city dweller in our fine country lands."

Mum and Vicky both shared a laugh at my expense.

"These are my lands too," I grumbled.

"No heels today?" Amusement pulled at Vicky's mouth. She'd promised not to tell anyone about my footwear disaster, but I could see the temptation on her face.

Mum glanced between us, eager to be let in on the joke. "What's that then?"

"Nothing," I said. "You lot just don't know good fashion."

"Says the woman in the orange tassel hat. And that coat."

"Oi, you, watch it," Mum said. "They're mine."

They both laughed, and Vicky resumed fanning out the shavings for the horse's bedding.

"Well, I'm very pleased to discover that the two of you are such tight friends," I deadpanned. "This should be a barrel of laughs."

"I knew you'd be a big grouch about it," Mum commented. "You and Cameron were always such mopers."

Cameron's face burned beneath my eyelids, and my heart squeezed. Sometimes the details of his features faded or blurred. Like a piece of him was being lost forever. I blinked his image away, noticing Vicky watching me, supporting her weight on her pitchfork.

When our eyes met, she glanced back at Mum. "You gonna put her to some real work, then?"

"Definitely. She's got a few years of making up to do." Mum's tone was light, but the words embedded themselves in my mind. *A few years of making up to do.* Like my struggles of the past few years were just something to be brushed away. It wasn't like I purposefully didn't visit because I was too busy or didn't care. It was because I couldn't bear it. I couldn't guarantee that I wouldn't crumble at the first mention of his name. I didn't want Mum and Dad to have to put me back together when they had to do that for themselves. I needed to be okay first.

But since I'd been home, the hurt had crept back in

like an old enemy, carving its place in my chest. The thought of my wonderful brother, so much life left to live…just gone. Gone. And for what? I'd thought I was ready, but it was a mistake to come back. It was too soon.

I could feel myself slipping, so I left to fetch another wheelbarrow.

"I'll start with the shit then, shall I?" I called, trying to keep my voice as mellow as possible. Tears threatened my eyes again, and all I wanted to do was scream into the wind until my lungs ached.

The cold lashed at me as I ducked outside, and the wind swirled my hair around my face.

I tried to push it down, the horrible ache building its way up my throat and spreading into my chest. But it grew. Squeezing. Suffocating the breath in my lungs.

Get it together, Holly. Get it together.

I sucked in some deep breaths, trying to calm my thundering heart. On the other side of the green fields, the horses were grazing and wandering around the pasture. The wind caught their manes, billowing it out like a shampoo advert on TV—but not an ad for one of Pertoni Clark's restyle shampoos. Those were very different. Batch tests resulted in half of users reporting unwanted colour changes. Mr Clark had suggested that was part of the lucky dip, but a few lawsuits said otherwise.

A white-and-grey speckled horse trotted along the fence, curious about me, or perhaps suspecting it was feeding time. I wondered which horse belonged to Vicky.

I focused on the animals, letting my breathing settle into rhythm. The grip on my chest loosened, and I let out a breath, feeling it in every fibre of my being. That was close. Too close to falling over the edge into the grief pit and not being able to climb back out.

I rolled the wheelbarrow along the uneven path and started shovelling shit into it.

There were only a few stray piles left, so I finished quickly. Mum and Vicky's laughter rang out from the stables behind me. *At least someone is having fun.* I paused at the gate to the horses' field, not feeling confident enough to enter just yet. The white horse from before spotted me and walked over, bucking its head slightly with each step. It hung its large neck over the gate and let out a whinny, flaring its nostrils.

"Hey there, girl. You look like a girl, anyway." I ducked my head to see the horse's underbelly. "Definitely a girl."

My hand twitched to stroke her, but I hesitated, not wanting to get bitten or get the gross horse smell under my now-chipped fingernails. Her deep dark eyes watched me, putting me on edge a little bit. *Is she judging me?* I wondered if I looked just as out of place to the horse as I felt. Even wearing Mum's disgusting orange tassel hat, I was an outsider. Even the horse knew. I sighed and took a tentative step forward.

"Do you ever feel like that?" I murmured softly. "Like you don't belong?" I shook my head. *I've been in the country for five minutes, and I'm already talking to horses again. Jesus. Mum would love that.*

The horse just looked back at me, because of course it did. It was a fucking horse.

"Time makes it better though, right? That's what they say—"

"How are you getting on?" Vicky's voice startled me, and I spun around to find her standing behind me, hands on her hips.

"Oh, yeah. Fine. I finished out here and was thinking about clearing the rest from the fields."

A smile pulled at Vicky's mouth. "Are you scared of them?"

Yes. "No. I was just saying hello first. Didn't want to trespass. I have to respect their home, don't I?"

She bobbed her head, her grin getting wider. "Is that why you were speaking to her? Trying to ask permission?"

Did she hear that? Oh, lord. I stood, my mouth open as I tried to find the words to explain what I was doing. But none came.

"It's cute. Not everyone understands how much they listen." She offered me a knowing smile and stepped forward. "I see you met Crystal. She's a rescue. Ex-racehorse." She rubbed her hands over the horse's face and tickled behind her long ears.

"Is she yours?"

"Yeah."

"I didn't know you wanted a horse."

Vicky brushed her fingers through Crystal's mane, tugging out a knot of hair. "Don't you remember how much I used to come up here with your mum and Biscuit? I know you were never too keen, but I used to love it." Her face fell, and her hand stilled for a moment. "After Cameron...your mum suggested I get my own. It gave her something to do, something to get up for... So I did. Your mum was right; Crystal saved me, too, in many ways. Gave me some purpose."

The air chilled around me. The sadness in Vicky's features tugged me forward. What did she remember when she thought about Cameron? Was it anything like how I felt? Guilt mixed with several other unnamed emotions flooded through me. I never wanted Vicky to feel like that. I should've been there for her. We should've been there for each other. This was my chance to reach out to her, to take that next small step.

"I'm sorry," I said, forcing myself to meet her gaze.

Vicky's blue eyes flicked to mine. "What?"

"I'm sorry," I said louder. "That sounds tough, and I should've been around more. I just...I just..."

"Holly, it's okay." Vicky brushed my arms, and I realised they were shaking. "You don't need to apologise."

"I do."

She took my hand in hers. "It's not your fault. What happened to Cameron. It was just a freak accident."

"Vicky, please...don't."

She studied me, and I cowered under her gaze, tears pricking my eyelids.

"Okay," she said, still holding my hand. She led us back to the gate. "You want to meet her properly?"

I nodded, relief washing over me with the change of subject. A cloud still hovered. I'd done the first step, so why didn't I feel much better?

Vicky laid my hand against Crystal's nose. When the horse didn't bite off my fingers, I relaxed a little, rubbing small circles on her long face. It was surprisingly soft.

"Look at you, mucking out, being at one with the animals. It's really nice," Vicky said. "Got to say those purple wellies look better than those heels you had on yesterday."

I snorted. Even comparing the two ironically was ridiculous.

"I'm serious," she said. "It's great to see you like this. Like how I remember."

The sincerity in her tone struck me. What memories did she hold close in her mind? Surely I wasn't that different from two years ago?

We were bound to change, and what was wrong with

not smelling like horse urine and looking like we'd been down the pit? London Holly was Holly 2.0. I dressed better, sure, but I could still have fun and pay homage to my country roots. As much as someone can when they lose their bestest friend in the whole world unexpectedly.

I flicked the tassels hanging from my hat. "I don't know. I don't think orange is really my colour."

Vicky laughed. "Yeah, maybe not the hat. It's pretty awful. Don't tell your mum that, though, she'll spear me on a pitchfork and display my head on top of the muckheap."

I grinned, some of the tension leaving my body. "I want to disagree, but yeah, she probably would."

Our eyes met, squeezing something in my chest. This wasn't ice though. This was warm. Warm and gooey and dangerous. And I was being sucked in.

"Would you be up for a little ride this afternoon?"

My mouth popped open. Ride? Petting one from behind the safety of a fence was one thing, but sitting on one of these giant running machines and trying not to fall to my death was something else entirely. I'd ridden with Mum a few times when I was younger, sure, but I could never shake the nervous feeling of impending doom. Plus, it'd been years since I'd even seen a horse, never mind tried to ride one.

"You don't have to, of course. I just thought it might be fun." Vicky smiled, but I could feel the challenge hidden underneath. A chance to prove myself—plus Mum would love it.

"Maybe a little one, then."

"Awesome." The cute dimple surfaced on her cheek. "Let's get you kitted up, though I'm not sure we'll have a helmet large enough for your big head."

"Hey! That's twice you've said that now." I jostled her, and she laughed. I loved how quickly we'd fallen back into our teasing habits. It proved we still had something.

Vicky led the way to the stables where Mum was waiting. She shot me a cheesy thumbs up as we neared, and all hope for getting through the Christmas holiday diminished immediately. Either through embarrassment or through being trampled to death, I might never make it back to London.

Chapter Ten

I couldn't understand how people found this enjoyable. My back hurt, my arse was numb, and I was scared for my life. To make things worse, I stunk of hay and excrement. A far cry from my usual crisp and clean designer wear in the city. The small victory was taking off the orange tassel hat, but its replacement wasn't much better: a riding hat with a Christmas-tree helmet cover stretched over it. Vicky swore it was the only one that would fit me, but I begged to differ. The way she cracked up seeing me wear it did ease the pain a little.

"Not half bad, Christmas Tree. Keep your back straight, hands on those reins," Vicky called, perusing me from the back of her own horse.

I think I preferred Princess. I readjusted my position,

the cumbersome back support pinching my sides, and squeezed my legs around Toffee's sizeable middle. He was a small, pudgy horse, with a scruffy golden coat. Small but mighty, Mum had called him, and both women promised he was a safe choice to ease me back into the saddle.

So far, he'd held steady as Vicky led me around the paddock with a guide rope.

Then when I was deemed horseworthy and on my own, the two of them had thought it funny to up the ante. I was determined to prove them wrong and impress Vicky. I was capable. After all, I had a country heart. I could do this.

Possibly.

"Okay, now stop," Vicky commanded.

I pulled on Toffee's reins and he slowed, plodding along before stopping with a big sigh. He looked over at the horses in the other fields, bucking his head slightly.

"Erm…why is he doing that?" I asked as Vicky trotted over to me on Crystal. She'd separated her blonde hair into two plaits on either side of her head. She looked adorable.

"Relax. It's just what they do to get rid of the flies." She pulled Crystal around so we were side by side. "You're looking good."

Even though she was probably joking, the compliment warmed my cheeks.

"You ready to step it up a notch?"

Toffee's ears twitched, making me nervous. *Is he side-eyeing me?* "I don't know…"

"You're doing great, sweetie!" Mum shouted from the other side of the fence.

A flash went off, and I turned to see her taking pictures. I groaned. *Why have I agreed to this?* I'd have to make sure those photos didn't end up on her social media. If my colleagues saw me with this stupid hat on, I'd never hear the end of it.

"Come on, Hol, live a little."

"I do live. I want to keep on living. That's the point."

Vicky shook her head, a smile tugging at her mouth. "Just a little trot around the perimeter. Nothing crazy."

"You've got me wearing this stupid hat. What more could you want?"

"There's a few things that spring to mind."

My stomach tightened. What did she mean by that? She'd said it so quietly, I wondered if I'd misheard her.

My phone rang, making me jump. Toffee sidestepped a few spots, taking advantage of the distraction. He turned his big behind towards Mum and brought me face-to-face with Vicky. I glanced at my watch to see Katie's name on the screen. *That's all I need right now.* I clicked reject and felt Vicky's stare on me, an unspoken question behind it.

"Sorry about that."

She smiled, but something else flashed across her features before she quickly masked it. "So how about a little trot?"

Vicky's sudden unease put me on edge. I wanted to make light of things again, to hear her lovely laugh.

"Come on, girls, what's taking so long?" Mum called. "I want to take a video for my Instagram!"

"Come on, Holly." Vicky pinned me with her gaze. "I dare you."

Her eyes held mine, full of something left unsaid. Was this a test of some sort? A chance to prove myself?

"Fine," I agreed, catching her look of satisfaction. "Just one lap, though. I can't feel my arse."

Without another word, she galloped off, kicking up dirt at Toffee and me. *Show off.* I squeezed my legs around the horse's middle and he plodded forward, with not even half as much grace or urgency as Vicky and Crystal.

I blew out a breath. *You can do this, Holly.* I kicked in my heels, trying to catch up. The strands of our last conversation echoed in my brain. What things did Vicky want? Did she think about us? Our first kiss? Or was I completely miles off?

Toffee picked up the pace, throwing me up and down in the saddle. I tried to remember the rise and fall rhythm, but every time I pressed my feet into the stirrups, the effort knocked me off balance.

"Vicky!" I called, but she was riding up ahead as we

circled the paddock. Toffee found a surge of energy from deep within and pushed onward, picking up speed. My foot slipped, and I tumbled forward in the saddle, the ground blurring underneath me.

This is it. This is how I die.

I tried to right myself, but the motion of the horse made it impossible. "Vicky! Wait!" I wrapped my arms around Toffee's neck, scrambling for the dropped reins. I found them, tugged, and Toffee skidded to a stop, throwing me off his back and catapulting me high into the air.

A haze of rain clouds distorted my vision before I landed on the floor with a hard thud. All the breath left my lungs. I tried to scream, but the sound stuck in my throat.

The last thing I remember was the hot searing pain flaring through my brain and the sound of Vicky's voice calling me deeper and deeper into unconsciousness.

Chapter Eleven

After rereading the same page three times, I rested the book on my bedside table. Mum had brought in a stack of her favourites to keep me occupied while I recovered, but they were much too racy and far too hetero for my liking. I shifted against the bedframe, pain shooting up my side. Bruised ribs and a sore head were not on my Christmas list to Santa this year, but without the body protector, it could've been a lot worse.

I pulled out my phone to check my messages. Since the trip to the hospital yesterday, Vicky had texted me multiple times to check I was alright. Now the messages had gone quiet, I wondered if she was questioning things as much as I was. The discomfort in my chest wasn't enough to distract me from our conversation on the horses. It pained me to admit it, but I thought Mum was right. There was something going on between us, and we needed to speak about it.

Small steps. That's what I had to remember.

I scrolled further down, my hand stilling over Cameron's name. I sucked in a shaky, painful breath and clicked it, my eyes flicking across the handful of undelivered messages. My fingers began to type.

Hey, Cam. Guess what? I fell off a horse yesterday and bruised my ribs, all while trying to impress Vicky Castleton. I know...I can just imagine your response. How much you'd tease me. How you'd roll your eyes and tell me it was about time the two of us got together. Maybe you just had a knack for seeing things about myself that no one else could. But I'm trying. I think I need to make this right. I'm just figuring out how to do that. I wish you were here to help me. You were always good at this sort of thing. I suck at it. Tears threatened my eyelids. *I miss you. I really, really miss you.*

I sent it, receiving the rebound message a few seconds later. The grip around my heart squeezed, and I let out a sob. Allowing myself to feel the loss for just a moment. The ache spread through my abdomen, the pain a thousand times more than any bruised rib could give me. I'd break every bone in my body if I could get my brother back. Even for a minute. Just so I could give him a hug and for him to tell me to stop being so silly. Tears spilled from my eyes.

I scrolled further up our messages, skipping over all the ones I'd sent him through the past two years until I saw his last reply in blue. I knew the words without reading them.

Skied an awesomeee red today. We'll defo have to come back next year. You'd love it. N can you tell Mum to stop liking all my posts plz? If not I'm gonna have to block her lol

Sometimes you do everything right. You wear a helmet and you stick to the piste. You know how to ski and can do so with confidence. But that doesn't stop someone from careening into you from behind, knocking you both into a tree. It doesn't stop them from surviving their mistake and you paying the ultimate price.

Sometimes you can do everything right, but it still goes wrong. Nothing in the world can protect you from that. One day you have a brother, and the next you don't.

I scrolled up further, reading our messages through blurred eyes. The grief washed over me, pulling me under. I couldn't fight it. Not today.

I tried to roll over, to tuck my knees to my chest and rock myself, but pain seared through my ribs, and I recoiled. I wrapped my arms around myself, squeezing. Trying to keep those broken pieces together. If I squeezed hard enough, maybe I could fix them. But I knew there would always be a missing piece. There would always be a hole in my chest.

So consumed with my thoughts, I didn't register the knock at the door until it opened. Vicky poked her head in, eyes widening when she saw me. She rushed in, hands immediately grasping my arms.

"Holly, are you okay? What's wrong? Is it the pain?"

I struggled to get the words out through my ragged breathing. I was too far gone to rein it in. Grief ate me from the inside, burning hot fire, devouring everything. *Cameron was dead. Cameron was dead.*

"Do you need to go back to hospital?" Vicky's blonde brows were furrowed, and she brushed a soothing hand through my hair. Her fingers were warm, the touch familiar.

I managed to shake my head, yet the concern in her features didn't disappear.

"Holly, please talk to me."

I couldn't look at her. Couldn't bear to see the pity in her stare. The way grief constructed barriers in the room. How it distanced people, keeping them in their own miserable, tear-dwelling quarters that ate them alive.

I sobbed, the ache stretching out and touching all the places I'd tried to lock down. The blackness behind my eyes swallowed me, imprisoning me from the inside.

Vicky caressed my face with her hand. The most gentle and heartfelt touch I'd ever experienced. "Breathe, Holly. In and out. Just breathe. It's okay. I'm here."

My eyes found Vicky's blue ones, deep and swirling with emotions I couldn't name. I blinked the tears away, letting them fall down my cheeks.

"Talk to me," she said.

"Cam—Cameron," I managed.

Her gaze crinkled, understanding washing over her features. I waited for the barrier, for her to step back and leave me to stew in my own sadness, hoping I'd pull myself out when I was ready.

Instead, she climbed onto the bed and opened up her arms, inviting me into her chest.

"Come here," she said softly.

I didn't hesitate, crawling into the warmth of her embrace and breathing in her familiar scent. She cradled me, her arms caressing mine, holding me as tight as my bruised ribs would allow. Her chin rested on my head, her steady breaths fanning over my hair, and for the first time in two years, I felt like I belonged somewhere.

Chapter Twelve

I woke to the same faded blue walls, beginning to get used to the sight of my childhood bedroom. What I wasn't used to was the feeling of Vicky's breathing and the gentle rise and fall of her chest. I registered her warm arms still wrapped around me, the two of us a cocoon of limbs. The moments before we fell asleep trickled back into my consciousness: Vicky witnessing my grief meltdown, her cradling me as I wept, the soothing sound of her heartbeat as I drifted into the safety of sleep.

Now that I'd awakened, snuggled into the curve of her body, I didn't want to move. It was the closest I'd been to her in years, but there was a deep familiarity there, as though we'd done this a million times before. I tilted my head back and let my gaze drift over Vicky's cute freckles, the long blonde eyelashes, the way her pink mouth rested in the depths of sleep. Warmth bloomed in my chest at the sight of so many admirable qualities in this woman I'd loved for so long. I still remembered the softness of her lips, even all these years later. I wondered what kissing her now might be like. A pulse awakened between my thighs at the thought of closing the distance and tasting her again.

We'd changed over the years, that was undeniable, but we were the same people who'd stayed up for hours talking and playing in the fields behind our houses. The same people who'd grown up together, sharing secrets and heartaches, good grades and bad grades, and enough laughter to last a lifetime. We were the same people who'd shared our first kiss under the pink light in Vicky's bedroom. Clumsy mouths and wandering hands, yearning for more but too scared to ask. Too scared to be. I wasn't scared any more. But was she?

I could definitely sense a barrier in the way her face would sometimes still, something crossing her mind as she hid behind a smile. I couldn't blame her. I wasn't sure I'd completely trust me, either. But I wanted to be better. I wanted to make it up to her.

Lying here with her, it felt like the barriers had dissolved, but I wasn't sure how long it would last. For the first time since I'd arrived, I dreaded going back to London. That realisation made me wrap my arms around her a little tighter.

Mum crashed through the door, wearing nothing but a skimpy red bikini.

Vicky jolted upright, taking me with her, and pain burned through my side.

"Jesus, Mother! What're you doing?" I wheezed.

"Oh god, I'm sorry." She covered herself with her hands. "I just needed an opinion, because your dad is useless when it comes to this stuff."

My eyes burned, not just from crying but from this image of my mother standing half-naked in my bedroom.

"Well, I think it looks great, Tracy," Vicky said a little sleepily.

"Thank you, love. It's for a spa weekend. Early Christmas present." Her eyes widened. "Ooh! I also bumped into Jeff this morning. He said to remind you to pop round. Something to do with a Christmas tree?"

Oh, no. I'd forgotten about my promise to Mr Simon. That was just what I needed.

When Mum didn't move to leave, I made a show of covering my eyes.

"Oh, Holly, don't be such a prude. We've all got the same bits."

I gawked at her. Please tell me this is a dream and Vicky Castleton is not witnessing this. "Mum, please. Can't you see I'm busy?"

Mum raised a dark eyebrow. "I can certainly see that.

What's going on here, then?"

We jumped away from each other, unaware that our limbs were still entangled. Pain shot through my chest again, and I grimaced. *Damn stupid ribs. Damn stupid horses.*

"Don't be pulling my leg now," Mum said, wagging a finger. "A mother always knows."

"Mum," I pleaded, heat searing my cheeks. I was transported back to my teenage years. I daren't even look at Vicky. This was mortifying.

"Alright, alright. I can take a hint." Mum headed out onto the landing, and Vicky sat up straight, unravelling herself from me.

Mum caught my eye in the doorway and patted her belly, mouthing "three grandchildren" before she closed the door.

Mortification level: 1000.

What could I even say after that? Vicky also seemed at a loss for words. She sucked in a deep breath and glanced at me before bursting out laughing.

I joined in too and winced, clutching my ribs. "Ow, ow!"

Vicky reached out to me without thinking, then pulled her arm away. "Are you alright?" she asked.

"Yeah, yeah, I'm fine."

She nodded slowly, sucking on her bottom lip. The movement drew my focus to her mouth, the idea of kissing her crossing my mind once again. Her blue eyes locked with mine. *She must feel this too, right?*

"Really, though. How are you?" she pressed.

"Better. Thanks for...before. I...I needed that." I held her gaze, despite every fibre in my body demanding I look away.

Vicky looked right back at me.

"I think I did too," she said quietly, her focus dropping to my mouth.

My heart rate galloped, a new type of tightness spreading through my chest. A shallow tingling sensation grew in my hands, and I itched to reach out and cup her face. To pull her close to me and kiss her, but I didn't want to break the moment. I didn't want her to ever stop looking at me like that.

"How often does it happen?" Vicky asked, tearing my attention from her Cupid's bow mouth.

How often did I feel like this? Honestly, not ever. Even my tumultuous relationship with Katie didn't have the same highs. Not in the same way, where electricity coursed through my veins, leaving me tingly everywhere. Where the connection ran so deep I could pick apart her mood by the look in her eyes or the twitch of her mouth. Honestly, I'd never felt about anyone the way that I'd felt about Vicky. She'd always been the one "what if" in my life. The regret. Maybe that's why I'd moved to London. It was my chance to finally move on.

But as I looked into those deep blue eyes of hers, I knew moving on wasn't what I wanted any more. I wanted her. I think I always had.

"Only with you," I said, finding the courage to place my hand on her thigh again.

"What?" Vicky's eyebrows drew together. "That's the first time that's happened?"

Wait a minute. "What do you mean?"

She hesitated, chewing over her words. "How upset you were before. The hyperventilating…that's the first time?"

Oh.

I stiffened, the blood pumping between my legs diverted to my face, sweeping away all the sexiness with it. "It happens sometimes, yeah." I made to move my hand away, but Vicky grabbed it.

"It was really horrible to see you like that, Holly. I'm worried about you. Are you talking to someone?"

And there it was. The inevitable words of concern… The pity stare, sucking all the life out of the room. And the air from my lungs. I didn't want to be a burden, weighing people down with my pain and sadness.

"I'm fine. I'm fine."

"You keep saying that, Holly. But do you really believe it?" Her gaze was piercing, daring me to brush it off. "Be honest with me."

I shook my head, feeling pinned into a corner. I

wanted to leave. I needed to get away before the feelings came clawing out of my chest and into my mind. The urge to run—I hated it. But Vicky's hand held me in place.

She squeezed it. "Talk to me."

So I did. For the first time since Cameron died, I opened up. Letting out some of the dark thoughts and the feelings I usually kept buried beneath the surface. Vicky sat and listened, rubbing her thumb over my fingers. She opened up too, about how looking after Crystal had been her own type of rehabilitation, and how she'd also been to speak with a counsellor.

"I'm not saying it solves all your problems. No one has the power to do that," she said, "but it stops you bottling it all up inside. I know you feel like you have to be the strong one, Holly. But you're a person too. You're only human. You're allowed to feel. To not be okay sometimes."

I gave her a small smile. "I hear you."

"Good." She looked down at our hands, resting entwined in her lap. "Despite everything, it's been really nice to see you. Really nice." She kept her head down, tracing my fingers softly.

"It's been really nice to see you too." I pleaded with her to look up. So I could read the emotion in her eyes and decide whether or not to kiss her. I so badly wanted to kiss her.

She opened her mouth to speak. "Holly, I…" She

sighed, her eyes flicking up to mine. "I...actually have another favour to ask you."

Her comment from yesterday rattled through my brain. *There's a few things that spring to mind.* "What is it?" I asked.

"Mum's got another stall at the Christmas Fair, but this one is in the city. I could use another pair of hands. If you're up for it, of course."

Spending more time with Vicky? As if I'd say no to that. "Sure. That sounds good. Although, I do have a favour to ask of you too."

She glanced up at me. "Intriguing. And what might that be?"

"You'll see." I grinned. "Gonna need to put those country muscles to some good use."

Chapter Thirteen

Vicky walked on ahead, wearing a red puffer coat with a faux-fur hood. A cluster of pigeons pecked at the frozen soil by her feet, scurrying away when she got too close. She bent down to inspect a shrivelled excuse for a Christmas tree and stood back up with a sigh. My gaze flicked away from her shapely, round bottom.

I pulled the list out of my pocket, eyes bulging as I read over the messy handwriting. "How is anyone supposed to meet these requirements three days before Christmas?" I muttered. "It's ridiculous."

"You know Mr Simon," Vicky said. "What did you expect?"

"When he said he needed help with the Christmas tree, I thought he meant decorating it or moving it. Maybe creating a Mabel-proof trap so the cat couldn't pull the damn thing over. Not to go fetch a tree with an equal number of branches on the left and the right, that's been grown in organic soil with no"—I squinted my eyes to read the next part—"squiggly bugs, and needles that are 1.25 inches long." I looked up at her, exasperated. "All we've got left here are trees on death row."

She spluttered, unable to contain the laughter.

"Vicky! Focus, please. He's never going to let me forget it."

"Relax. You're the one that gets to go gallivanting back to London. I'm the one that has to live on the same street as him. I'll never hear the end of it."

A jolt flashed through me. That was the second time she'd said something like that. Did she want me to stay too?

I looked at her, trying to make something of her expression. "Actually, I've been thinking about it…and I'm going to stay until New Year's Day," I said.

Her expression sharpened. "Are you? I thought you said you were driving back Boxing Day?"

"Well…I changed my mind. Finalised it this morning."

A genuine smile lit up her face, one that made tingles dance in my stomach. "That's really great."

I hoped she meant it. I thought so too. I'd had so much fun reconnecting with Vicky, it seemed a shame to cut it short. I had no reason to return home anyway. Working for Mr Clark had real benefits when it came to holiday entitlement, and I usually had some left over. Returning on Boxing Day was just a self-preservation safety date for myself. Seeing Vicky react in this positive way definitely gave me some hope that she could still have feelings for me too.

Her gaze held mine until a yell made us both turn our heads.

"Morning, ladies," Harry said, righting himself before almost stumbling again over a pile of logs lying on the gravel. He was the fifth generation to own the Christmas tree farm in Mistleberry, and by far the clumsiest. He brushed off his dirty hands on his black trousers. "Find anything to your fancy?"

"Not really," Vicky told him, making a show of browsing the awful collection.

I glanced at the nearest row of trees, barely even a foot tall. Nowhere near the specified 5.7 feet Mr Simon requested. Harry's Christmas tree farm was seriously lacking in the Christmas tree department.

"To be frank, I am a bit surprised to see you here so close to Christmas," Harry said. "Everything's gone." He ran a hand through his long ginger beard before turning to me. "Not seen you in a few years, young 'un. Sorry to hear about your brother."

"Thanks." I bobbed my head. The ache of Cameron's

death simmered lower with every new mention. Or perhaps the close proximity to Vicky made it easier to swallow. She had that effect on me, like everything was going to be alright.

I ducked my head into my coat, hiding away from the cool morning breeze. "So you don't have anything else available?"

"What about that one?" Vicky pointed over my shoulder at a small cluster of trees bordered off by a wire fence.

"Oh, no. I'm sorry, ladies. Those are reserved."

I raised an eyebrow. "Reserved? For who?"

His eyes lit up. "The Joneses."

"Who?" I glanced at Vicky, but she looked away, a strange expression on her face. Weird.

"You don't know the Joneses? That's who's been building on those fields behind your estate. The ones that've bought the cinema and who are renovating the village. They're millionaires."

Ah, so they're Mr and Mrs Moneybags, then. Mum had mentioned the amount of changes proposed at the village meeting.

"Maybe I could speak with them," Vicky offered. "I'm sure they'd understand."

"Sorry, girls." Harry held up his big meaty hands, knocking a pencil from his top breast pocket. "I'm not allowed to give out their personal information. They'd shut me down faster than you can say *Vogue*."

Vogue? "Well, maybe I could tweet them or something?" I suggested. "Millionaires like Twitter…er, X, right?"

He quirked his thick, ginger eyebrows. "Oh, do you know bird calls? Those damn pesky pigeons keep trying to nest in my roof. And dropping special *parcels* all over the place." He scowled at a few nearby pigeons as they pecked stray bits of gravel.

That wasn't quite what I meant—but still. "I know, right? I hate those birds. Stupid flying turdbags." Both of them looked at me, surprised by my outburst. "What? I do. I hate them."

"Well, if you can get rid of my pest problem, maybe we could work something out."

You've got to be kidding me.

"You want us to get rid of the pigeons for you?" I asked.

Vicky swatted my arm. "Hey, don't rope me into this."

I grimaced, pain shooting down my side. Vicky apologised, but I waved off her concern. *Damn ribs.* "How do you expect me to do that, exactly?"

Harry shrugged. "Beats me."

"Wait." Vicky grabbed my shoulder. "Doesn't Pertoni Clark have a bird repellent device? I've seen it on TV."

"The walking scarecrow thing?" I tried to recall exactly how useful the device had been during testing. "From what I remember, they had some problems with it. Recalled some devices because of malfunctions."

"How so?"

"The robots were embedded with AI, and they were coming out with all sorts of things. Plus the usual fire hazards."

"Could you get one?"

I bit my lip. Products that were pre-release should be stored in the warehouse. But I wasn't sure if there were any near here. It was possible. "Maybe."

"Really?" Harry asked.

"She works for Pertoni Clark."

"No way! I'm such a huge fan of his. The chainsaw gloves changed my life." He jumped up, beaming like a schoolgirl meeting their crush. The idea of the large and clumsy Harry wielding chainsaw gloves made me swallow. How had he not cut off any limbs yet? My gaze dropped to his hands. He did actually have the end digit of his ring finger missing. All things considered, I'd say that was a win for him.

"I could make a few calls." Dani sure owed me a couple of favours. Using my car as a secret chocolate spot was one of them.

Harry smiled, showing his gap-toothed grin. "That would be great. You do that and the tree is yours."

I pulled my phone from my jeans pocket and dialled Dani's number. It turned out there was a warehouse in Frostchester, just an hour away, so Vicky and I could pick it up on the way to the Christmas Fair tonight.

"How's it going with Bedroom Girl?" Dani asked.

"That's the least catchy nickname ever."

I could practically hear her roll her eyes down the phone. "Whatever. You know who I mean. Stop deflecting. How's it going with her?"

I glanced over at Vicky, who was having an animated exchange with Harry over by the main building. Her blonde curls framed her face perfectly. The sweet sound of her laugh carried over their conversation, squeezing something in my chest.

"She's good. It's going good."

"Good, huh? Sounds exhilarating. If I didn't know better, your good is someone else's amazingly perfect head-over-heels in love."

I shook my head. "Shut up. You don't know what you're talking about."

"I know everything. Remember: don't count the days, make the days count."

"What bus advertisement have you stolen that from?"

She laughed. "It was a quote my dad had up in his gym. It used to motivate him to train, but it works for life too."

After a few more teasing jokes at my expense, Dani hung up the phone, agreeing to organise with the Frostchester warehouse, even though she was on her Christmas break. Promising her some more KitKats seemed to do the trick.

I walked back down the gravel path to join the others. Vicky looked up at me when I approached, her eyes sparkling. I'd never seen such light in someone's eyes before. I wanted her to always look at me like that.

This was my chance to make up for it. Small steps, just like Dad said.

"All sorted?" she asked, squeezing my arm.

"Yep." It seemed a lot of effort to get Mr Simon the tree of his dreams, but if it meant spending more time with Vicky, it was worth it. Getting revenge on the pigeons was an unexpected Christmas present.

"You know, we could run past the ice-cream place on the way back, get a scoop each." She nudged my shoulder. "Just like old times?"

We'd done that together with Cameron a lot. I grinned at the memory. "Ice cream? In the dead of winter?" I teased.

She winked. "Never a bad time for ice cream, Hol."

I felt another tugging in my abdomen. Ice cream in the winter. Bantering with Vicky. Being back home. It almost felt like I could reclaim parts of what I'd lost.

"Let's go then." I smiled at her, feeling more like myself than I had in a long time.

Chapter Fourteen

It took us an hour, but with the robot scarecrow safely in the car, Vicky and I arrived at the City Hall to set up for the Christmas Fair. The collection of the robot had gone better than expected; the only downside was the assembly process, which we'd have to brave tomorrow. Constructing a robot scarecrow with Vicky Castleton was not what I'd expected to be doing on Christmas Eve Eve. Oddly, I was excited by it.

The Christmas market was easily ten times bigger than our little village fair. The city had provided their own tables for the sellers, making it less cumbersome than before for us to set up. The permanent craftspeople and food sellers were stationed in mini wooden cabins, with fairy lights, and Christmas greetings sprayed on the sides.

The combined scents of spiced mulled wine and sweet cinnamon made me salivate as we found our table. A huge Ferris wheel sat beside City Hall, sparkling and flashing with red and green lights. Joyful Christmas music drifted through meticulously placed speakers. I felt like I was stepping right into a cheesy Christmas movie.

I wasn't quite sure why Vicky had needed my help. My bruised rib was healing but rendered me pretty useless with carrying anything of real weight. It did give me the opportunity to admire her strong biceps, though, while I followed behind with a light box of stuffed toys.

We set up stall next to a lovely Asian woman called Nadia, who was selling handcrafted dreamcatchers, colourful crystals and delicate wooden ornaments. She welcomed us both with a hug and took a genuine interest in what we were selling.

The city was heaving. People were either dashing about purchasing last-minute Christmas gifts or else spending the evening browsing with friends and warm wine. The two groups were easily categorised by the speed of movement and the level of panic on their faces. Luckily, I'd sorted all my presents a month in advance. All except for one. I needed to get Vicky something.

Normally, I'd jump to buy something expensive. A ring or a necklace or something sparkly. But it felt wrong for Vicky. It needed to be personal.

We barely had a chance to talk because it was so

busy. The embroidered journals, in particular, were a hit, along with the knitted stuffed animals. The terrible cow bag Vicky had stitched herself remained untouched, something I teased her about whenever I got the chance.

It surprised me how much I enjoyed chatting with the customers. In my job, I was heavily involved behind the scenes, so it made a nice change. Where I could be a little stilted, Vicky was a natural. I thought she'd be very successful in advertising. The idea of Vicky working with me at Pertoni Clark made me feel all flustered. It was a possibility, and it made a future with her plausible—if she was interested, of course. If only Mr Clark could make a mind-reading device that wasn't likely to catch fire, that would be great.

The evening grew colder and darker, but the crowd's spirits never waned. Children scampered by with candyfloss and chocolate Santas, adults with steaming mulled wine or brandy hot chocolates. The atmosphere stayed electric, and we'd almost sold out of all our stock.

"This is amazing," Vicky said. "Mum is going to be so pleased."

"You're quite the salesperson. Who'd have thought?"

She turned to me and raised an eyebrow. "And what is that supposed to mean?"

I looked at her—really looked at her—seeing both versions of the Vicky Castleton I adored. The quieter, caring Vicky still lived on behind the surface of the confident and sexy woman she'd grown into. Emotions stirred in my chest, and I shook my head. "Nothing. You're just very…you."

She snorted. "You work in advertising and that's the best you can come up with?" she teased. "I'm surprised Pertoni Clark hasn't gone under."

I picked up the sad cow bag. "You're a better salesperson than you are at knitting."

Vicky jabbed me, and I grimaced. Her face immediately crumpled. "I'm sorry, Hol. I keep forgetting about your ribs." The corner of her mouth twitched. "Although you are annoying and probably deserve it."

"Charming."

She burst into laughter. "I've missed this," she said, shooting me a smile that flew straight into my heart.

"Me too." Everything felt easy with Vicky. It was almost as if the last two years hadn't happened. In order to move forward, though, I needed to put all my cards on the table. Unless…I glanced at the other stalls, searching for a sprig of mistletoe. That'd certainly be the easier option. She couldn't misunderstand that gesture.

And I really wanted to kiss her.

"You want to have a look around?" Vicky asked. "We've more than exceeded what I thought we'd sell, and the food smells bloody amazing."

"Sure, that sounds nice." She started to pack away,

but I held a hand up. "But first—I'd like to do something."

I handed the cow bag to her, and she frowned. "I'm not going to bin it."

I laughed. "No! We couldn't bin such a masterpiece. It's an original Vicky Castleton, after all."

She eyed me suspiciously. "What are you up to?"

"I'm not sure why you think so poorly of me. I'd just like to give him a home."

"You want to buy it?"

"I do."

She broke into a smile. "But I thought you hated it."

"How could I hate something that's so characteristically you?"

"I don't know if I should take that as an insult or a compliment, so I'm just going to say…SOLD! To the lady with the fancy coat and the bruised rib."

We packed up and loaded the car before heading back into the market, re-energised and feeling lighter than air. We browsed some of the stalls. Vicky picked up a cute reindeer hat and a handmade bookmark, while I tried to find something I could gift her for Christmas. I considered getting her some of the handmade jewellery, but it didn't feel quite right. *Also, where is that damn mistletoe?*

After buying two freshly made crêpes, sugar for me, and chocolate and strawberry for Vicky, we strolled down the market towards the big Ferris wheel, Vicky linking her arm with mine. Warmth spread through me at the touch;

it was a small gesture that echoed another time, as though the years that had passed and distanced us had shrunk and fallen away.

We sat on a wooden bench beside a young dad and a son, who was wielding a flashing lightsabre like a young Jedi.

"So your mum's pretty good at crafting, and you're pretty good at selling," I said. "Have you thought about turning it into a proper business?"

She nodded, still chewing. "It's definitely crossed my mind a few times. I just…I don't know."

"What is it?"

She sighed, wiping her mouth on a napkin. "It's just different doing it in the holidays and doing it full-time. It's…scary. What if it tanks? I'm not sure I'm ready."

"Any change is scary. But you've got a good chance. Mr Clark always enthuses about the importance of a product that will sell. And from what I've seen, you've already got that. Next step is doing a business plan. If it's what you want to do, you should go for it."

"It's not that simple. There's other people that I need to think about. It's…complicated." She seemed to consider it. "Plus, I don't know if Mum would even want to do it full-time…but I will think about it, thanks."

"No problem."

"What about you? You think you'll ever move back to Mistleberry?"

The thought had been playing on my mind for the last few days. I'd felt less lonely and more myself, and spending time with my family was helping heal the spaces in my chest.

I pursed my lips, making a show of thinking. "Never say never."

"Interesting." She grinned at me, and my eyes were drawn to her dimple. "Fancy a ride on the wheel?"

A romantic view of the city sounded like a perfect place to make a move.

I paid for two tickets, and we stumbled into the rickety cabin. It swung gently as we got ourselves comfortable, and I tried to squash the fear that shot up my spine. The wheel started moving, carrying us higher above the twinkling lights.

You can do it, Holly.

"This is awesome," I said, a little breathless, peering through the glass at the bustling city below us.

"Are you still afraid of heights?" Vicky asked, her thigh brushing against mine.

I tried not to think about the heat of our bodies and focused on her question. "I wouldn't say I'm overjoyed being so high above the ground, but I can overlook it when the view is this beautiful. Just don't put me on a glass ledge."

"Is it weird that I'm happy about that?"

I turned to her, surprised by her tone, and found a

solemn look on her face. "What do you mean?"

"I'm just happy you're still in there underneath the expensive clothes and the busy lifestyle." She nudged me and smiled, but it didn't quite touch her eyes. "For a while, I didn't know."

That wasn't the first time she'd said something like that. "I'm still me, you know. I think you'd quite like the city. There's lots going on."

"I'm not sure. I don't think I'm a fan of the fast life."

"You afraid of finally being around more people than cows?" I teased. "I'd like to say the smell is better, but I'd be lying."

She looked down at the floor, shifting underneath my gaze. "I don't hate the city. I actually have considered it…It's just complicated. It's a big change, a big commitment. I don't know. It's probably silly." She shook her head, her hair falling across her face. "You…you're just different, but also the same. Do you know what I mean? I know I've joked with you about it, but really all this time, I just…missed you."

My heart thumped faster in my chest. I wasn't sure if it was from the height or from the air thickening in the cabin. When Vicky's eyes met mine, I knew the answer. Now was my chance. "I missed you too. Vicky…I…" I swallowed, my throat suddenly dry. I closed my eyes briefly, trying to remember the words I wanted to say to her. *Small steps, Holly. Just say it.*

I looked back at her, into those blue eyes that always seemed to see right into my soul. The same eyes I'd leaned into when we had our very first kiss all those years ago.

"I'm sorry, Vicky. For the way I acted when we were younger." Now that the first words were out, the rest followed quickly. "I was terrified of my feelings for you. I didn't know how to deal with them, so I pushed them away and ran, and that meant I pushed you away too. I think in some ways I've been running from things for a long time. My feelings for you...what happened with Cameron...and now my family too. But I don't want to keep running. I can't."

Surprise flashed across Vicky's features, pulling her brows closer together. "Holly, listen—"

"It doesn't stop me from feeling. It all catches up with me eventually, and it all piles on top of me like a crushing weight. But just because I moved and tried to stay busy, it doesn't mean I ever stopped feeling things for you. And that kiss...our first kiss. It means a lot to me. So do you. I think about it all the time."

My stomach twisted with nerves I hadn't felt since I was a teenager. I willed Vicky to say something, forced myself to look at her, and found sad eyes already watching me. *Oh, no. She's going to reject me.*

Vicky swallowed. "You mean a lot to me too, Hol. Something I don't think any amount of running or distance between us could change."

"Really?"

She nodded. "Of course. You were my first love. Nothing will ever erase that."

My mind caught on the past tense. Nausea rolled through my belly. "You were mine too. You still are."

Vicky's mouth dropped, her gaze flicking over my face. "What?"

The wheel slowed to a stop as our cabin reached the top, gently rocking us back and forth. I glanced out of the window behind Vicky. The city stretched out as far as I could see, twinkling lights covering the darkness like sparkling glitter.

My heart hammered in my chest. "There hasn't been a day where I didn't think about you. I was a coward. And I'm still learning to be brave. To own my actions and go after what I want." I placed my hand on her thigh, and Vicky let out a soft gasp. So much had changed between us, but I felt the electricity in the air. That hadn't changed. My feelings hadn't. Had hers?

Vicky's gaze dropped to my lips, and I knew then. She felt this too. I slid a hand behind her neck, tangling my fingers in her hair. My breath caught in my throat. I wanted to savour every moment, to commit it to memory. To never run away from it.

I leaned closer, so close I could taste her sweet breath on my lips.

"Holly…" she said softly.

I pressed my lips to hers, and everything in my body set alight. Every twinkling Christmas light and firework combined together and burst through my veins. It all came crashing back to me. The night in her bedroom, her soft mouth, her sweet taste, how every cell in my body came to life.

"Stop." She pulled back and put a hand to her lips.

Everything inside me shrivelled and turned cold.

"I can't do this," she said.

My hands fell to my lap. The wheel groaned as it started to descend.

Everything felt like ending. I was too late. Too much time had passed. Vicky couldn't forgive me. But I had to try.

"I know one apology isn't going to cut it, Vicky. But it's a start."

She shook her head. "No, Holly…it's not that." Her word came out slow and choked. Her eyes glossed over. "I have a girlfriend."

Chapter Fifteen

I stared at the stupid robot scarecrow in its stupid Pertoni Clark box, cursing myself for this stupid situation I'd gotten myself into.

A week ago, I was fine—I wasn't great, I'll admit that, but I was fine. In the space of a week, I'd fallen under Vicky Castleton's spell for the second time, and now my heart had been turned inside out.

I was mixed parts angry and sad. Sad that this…thing I had going with Vicky couldn't go anywhere. Angry that she never thought to mention the fact she had a girlfriend. Not just any girlfriend, but Tanya Jones—the drop-dead gorgeous catwalk model who'd featured in many fashion magazines, including *Vogue*. The Tanya Jones whose family had bought the land behind our houses where we used to play as kids, planning to demolish the greenery and turn it into more houses. The Tanya Jones who was freakin' loaded and beautiful and probably pissed liquid gold.

I wanted to scream, and cry, and burn every piece of designer clothing I had just to send a message. A message that I was angry…but mostly just sad.

And now I had to take this stupid robot scarecrow to Harry's Christmas tree farm, all so Mr Simon could get his perfect tree. I couldn't see the point any more. My Christmas spirit had been truly flushed down the toilet.

I'd been sitting on the bottom step like a misbehaving child, contemplating every decision I'd made in my life. I sighed and forced myself to stand and put on my boots. "I'm off out now, Mum!" I called down the hallway.

"Okay, love." I heard a clatter of porcelain on the table, and the door squeaked open. Butterbee scampered along the laminate flooring, greeting me like she hadn't just seen me an hour ago. Her wagging tail and wiggling bum drew a small smile from me.

Mum poked her head around the door, grimacing. "How are you feeling?"

"I'm fine."

"I'm sorry. If I'd known, I'd have said something."

"I know, Mum. It's okay."

Mum had been just as shocked as me when I told her

about Vicky's girlfriend, and now she felt guilty for getting my hopes up. I didn't blame her; how Vicky had managed to keep this such a secret was a surprise to me. Then again, did she really owe me an explanation? I just didn't want to talk about it any more. Mum's fussing around me only made me feel more pathetic.

Without another word, I picked up the box and left through the front door. I struggled to carry it, mild pain flaring through my ribs, but I pushed through. Vicky's car wasn't outside her house, and a pang of jealousy shot through my chest. I'd assumed she wouldn't come to help me after the events of last night, but the absence of her car and the thought of her with the beautiful Tanya Jones made me just want to cry right there in the street.

Whatever. I don't need her.

Mum would've offered to help if I'd asked. But I couldn't handle any more of the pity stares as it was. I'd never been a fan of DIY or manual things. I was more brain than brawn. But how hard could it be to assemble a robot scarecrow? Right?

I groaned and cursed Dani. This could all be traced back to her. Why did I ever agree to come back in the first place?

I drove over to Harry's farm, blaring Wham's "Last Christmas" loud through the speakers. As I turned into the dirt car park, my heart skipped a beat.

Vicky leaned against her car. She'd come.

Her arms were wrapped around herself, and she was snuggling into a warm blue coat I hadn't seen before. *What is she doing here?*

I sighed, reluctantly turning down the volume of my heartbreak Christmas ballad, and stepped out of the car. The winter wind nipped at my face, nearly taking the door off its hinges.

"What're you doing here?" I asked.

"I said I'd help you." Vicky attempted a smile. "And nice to see you too."

"You didn't have to." I opened the rear door to my BMW, and as I attempted to retrieve the box, the wind blew it onto my legs, pushing me inside. I hit my head on the passenger seat while the door tried to trap my leg in the hinges.

"Are you alright?" Vicky pulled me back out, trying to suppress a laugh. "It's windy up here, isn't it?"

"Mmm." I couldn't look at her without feeling prickles behind my eyelids. I turned away, dragging the box out of the back. *Swallow it, Holly. Push it down. You'll be fine. You'll be fine.*

"Holly, can we talk, please?"

"Why are you here?" I heaved the box up and started making my way towards the farm a short walk away. Vicky followed me.

"I said I'd help. And I knew you wouldn't let me come with you if I asked."

"Well, I don't really want to talk right now."

"Okay, just let me help you then." She grabbed the end of the box, easing the weight. I let her help me carry it, for lack of a reason not to. I'd already felt like a child earlier today, and I hated feeling inadequate and useless.

The wind whipped my hair around my face, blowing strands into my mouth. I tried to spit them out, but it was futile.

We passed through the large metal gates, already left open for our arrival, and walked down the gravel path.

"I'm sorry, okay? I should've told you sooner. I know I should have. There just didn't seem to be a good time."

"And you think this is?"

"Sometimes there's never a good time, is there?"

We lowered the box onto the ground, both mildly out of breath. Vicky's black beanie hat was lopsided, and I fought the urge to reach out and correct it. She sighed, her face softening. *Did she have to look so cute?*

I looked down at the floor, avoiding her gaze. "Just forget it. It's fine."

She hesitated. "It's clearly not."

"Well, I wished you'd told me about it sooner, but you hardly owe me any explanations about your life now, do you?" I somehow kept bitterness from creeping into my tone. "I'm sorry if I made you feel uncomfortable."

She shook her head, reaching out to me. "Holly,

come on…that's not the case. And I'm sorry I didn't tell you. It's just complicated and new and you—"

I lifted a hand, feeling thoroughly defeated but determined not to lose the last shred of pride I still had. "It's fine. Really, I get it. Let's just leave it. I'll go back to the city soon, then I'll be out of your hair. Easier for everyone, right?"

Crunching footsteps down the path caught our attention as Harry made his way towards us. The cool wind howled around me, trying to tug at my coattails and drag me away. I wished it were that simple. Mr Simon better appreciate this damn tree.

"Hello, ladies. How's it going?"

"Great," I answered, not meaning for it to come out so sarcastically. I cleared my throat. "I've got the robot here. It just needs a little setting up."

"Wonderful! I can't wait to get rid of those bloody things." Harry rubbed his hands together. "Do you want some help?"

"We're good—"

"That'd be great—"

Vicky and I spoke together. I narrowed my eyes at her. Why did she want us to be alone? Harry and I could sort this just fine. I didn't want to speak about it any more. It was humiliating.

He glanced between us, rubbing a hand over his beard. "Oh, er, I don't want to get in the middle of something…I got three daughters, and I learned it's best to stay out of it where I can." He hovered for a moment, allowing one of us to answer. When we didn't, he shrugged and pointed a badly bruised thumb over his shoulder. "You know where to find me if you need me."

We stood awkwardly, listening to the sound of his footsteps retreating. Two pigeons flew over to inspect the box, their beady eyes examining me.

"I should've said something about Tanya, I'm sorry. I just didn't want to lose you again when I've just got you back. Things with us have always been complicated, and I didn't want to scare you away." Vicky sniffed and turned around. I grabbed her shoulder, trying to spin her, but she resisted. "I don't want to get upset," she said, holding her fingers under her eyes before facing me. "But I've loved spending this time with you, Hol. It feels so good to have you back in my life. I don't want to lose that." Her voice broke, and she hung her head, a few stray tears escaping down her cheeks. "I don't want to lose you again."

Something squeezed in my chest. I hesitated for a second before pulling her into me, wrapping my arms around her. "You're not going to lose me. Okay? You never could. It's not possible."

She hugged me back, and the two of us stayed like that for a few minutes, the wind whistling around us. I breathed her in, letting her smell comfort me like a blanket. I didn't want to lose her, either. But could we be just friends?

My gut twisted at the thought. Our families had planned to get together tonight for Christmas Eve food and drinks. Did that mean Tanya would be there too?

Vicky pulled back. Her blue eyes were red and glossy with tears. "I'm sorry for getting emotional about it. But it's been so good to have you home. I didn't realise how much I'd missed you."

"I've missed you too." I forced myself to meet her gaze. *Don't look at her mouth. Don't look at her mouth.* The memory of our kiss sent lightning through my veins and heat through my stomach. I wanted to do it again. But I couldn't. That realisation made my heart sink. Just friends. That seemed impossible.

Needing a distraction, I pulled a pair of scissors from my pocket and stabbed them into the cardboard box by our feet. "Right, let's get started then, shall we?"

***

An hour, three pigeon attacks, and two paper cuts later, the robot scarecrow was up and running and already causing havoc. Harry seemed to love it, though. He clapped and cheered every time it wheeled over to a group of birds, shouting insults which he'd recorded.

"Well done, ladies. It's the best gift I've ever received. I wish I could give you more trees for it." He heaved our tree up onto his shoulder, and we followed him to his van. He'd agreed to bring the tree back with us to Mr Simon's, saving me from strapping it to my car. Something I couldn't do to my BMW. Not even if it meant Mr Simon and Mabel haunted me every day over my failings.

"Get outta here, you scabby ratbirds!" The scarecrow wielded its plastic arms and hurtled towards a group of pigeons. "I see you there too. Little furry maggots!" It wheeled over to the reception building, extended its small head with the camera inside, and resumed its manic waving. It was working, though, and the path from the reception up to the trees was already bird-free.

"Ah, it's really top-notch. Really is." Harry's eyes lit up as he turned to us, nearly taking off both our heads with the tree on his shoulder. "I tell you what. I'll name him after you."

"What?" I looked at him, dumbfounded, but he only grinned wider, obviously pleased with whatever his brain had cooked up.

"Victrolly! Get it? He's on wheels, and it's both of your names."

I tried to mask the disgust I felt at being associated with that thing. "Oh…right. That's nice."

Vicky couldn't hold it, though, and burst out laughing. "I think that's the best thing I've heard in ages, Harry." She slapped him on the back, and he joined in the laughter.

"I can even get her a name badge to wear. Like this." He thumbed the one pinned on his mucky shirt with pride.

I glanced at Vicky, unable to stop the smile creeping onto my face. This week was so bizarre, my emotions were all over the place. I didn't know whether to laugh or cry or scream up at the grey skies above.

"Get outta here, bird brains!" Victrolly shouted. That drew a laugh from the three of us as we headed into our cars, and get outta there we did.

Chapter Sixteen

Mr Simon's house hadn't changed in all the years I'd known him. He was a meticulous man and liked things to have order. Everything in his house had a label attached to it, confirming what everybody already knew: that the TV remote was in fact the TV remote, and the box of tissues on the coffee table was in fact a box of tissues. The table even had a label in case someone was confused over its purpose in the house—but you get the idea. I was surprised he hadn't stuck one to Mabel—*Cat.*

Harry helped the tree into the designated space Mr Simon had cleared out for it, shooting us a cheeky chuckle as he left, adding on, "Cya, Victrolly".

Vicky seemed to be as amused as I was, taking in Mr Simon's surroundings, but I guess it couldn't hurt to be organised. Maybe I could give Dani a label-maker for Christmas instead—the woman could use it.

"She's a beauty." Mr Simon gawked at the tree now standing in the centre of his living room and whipped out a ruler—also labelled *ruler*—from his back pocket. He measured the pine needles, nodded with a satisfactory grunt and then slipped it back into his trousers. "Simply perfect. I can't thank you enough."

He grinned, revealing his crooked and pointy teeth. The smile was genuine and made him seem younger. Warmth spread through my chest and I nodded, very surprised with how the day had turned out so far. I looked over at Vicky, and flutters gathered in my stomach.

Now, that reaction's not ideal, but I could work on it.

Mr Simon's demeanour changed. He wrung his hands, standing awkwardly between us, looking at the boxes. "I don't suppose you'd like to stay and help me decorate, would you? If it's not too much bother?"

I hadn't got any plans for tonight, so I nodded. "Sure, I'm happy to do that." I caught Vicky looking at her phone before she replied the same. Was she texting Tanya?

Ugly jealousy swirled inside. You've no right to be jealous, Holly. Vicky isn't yours. She never was.

But that isn't how it felt. Vicky had been such a huge part of me for as long as I could remember. The idea of her with someone else—never mind the gorgeous, wealthy Tanya, made me want to join Victrolly in running around the farm, screaming at the pigeons.

"Are you sure?" Mr Simon scratched at his beard. "I don't want to cause any fuss."

I smiled. Of course he thought this was fuss but that finding a Christmas tree with needles 1.25 inches long two days before the big day wasn't. "I like decorating," I told him. "And my mum has already done it this year, so...all good with me."

He nodded. "Would you like an eggnog?"

"Sounds perfect."

"I'll be back in a jiffy."

When he returned, we were already picking baubles out of the clearly labelled boxes. He nearly dropped the eggnog glasses on the floor.

"Oh, girls. I have a...certain routine for doing things...I...erm..."

Vicky put a comforting hand on his arm. "It's okay. You want to show us the way you usually do it?"

He nodded, sucked in a deep breath, and had a sip of his drink.

The ease with which Vicky recognised his discomfort warmed me. She was so sweet like that. I didn't always know what to say or do in a situation, but Vicky just oozed empathy and comfort. The memory of her wrapped around my body when she cradled me to sleep made me swoon momentarily; it had felt like a dream to be close to her in that way.

Mr Simon swiped a tissue from the table and wiped the eggnog off his moustache. "Okay, girls, listen carefully. I'll show you how the Simons decorate a Christmas tree."

It was a strict process, and both Vicky and I received multiple telling-offs for bad tinsel placement or wonky ornaments, but we finished the tree, and to Mr Simon's credit, it was beautiful. I'd even convinced him to play some Christmas music to set the mood. It wasn't my choice, but he had a favourite Christmas carols collection, which he played on his old record player.

Now we were on miscellaneous decoration duty. Armed with tinsel, Vicky leaned closer to a picture and inspected it.

"That's me and our Mabel when she was a kitten," Mr Simon gushed. I wondered if he'd labelled the photo frame.

"It's a lovely picture," Vicky commented. When she placed it down, I smiled as I spotted that he had, in fact, labelled it too. She circled the picture with some red tinsel, trying to keep it even.

Mr Simon ushered us over to the fireplace, where there were dozens of matching photo frames, each with a picture of Mabel. I found his obsessive behaviour endearing, perhaps seeing him for the first time. Had he always been like this, and I'd never paid enough attention? I softened, remembering Mrs Simon's death over fifteen years ago. They'd never had children, and Mabel had been his companion ever since. I scanned the pictures, searching for one of Mrs Simon. I didn't remember much about her, only that she had wild, curly hair and was always smiling.

Without thinking, I asked, "Do you have any pictures of Mrs Simon?"

Even though the Christmas carols were still playing through the speakers, there was an awkward feeling about the room. I immediately regretted opening my mouth.

Mr Simon froze, his back to me, arm extended in bauble adjustment. His head dropped briefly. "No, dear. I don't." He was quiet for a while, and I assumed the conversation was over. He straightened the red bauble on the tree and sighed. "It's just me and Mabel now, so…"

"I'm sorry," I said. "I shouldn't have said anything."

He waved his hand. "No, no. It's alright. You're not the first person to ask." He retrieved another bauble from the box and measured across the branches with his ruler before settling on an appropriate placement. "I couldn't look at her pictures. It just made me too sad. Reminded me of everything I'd lost. I like to look at Mabel… She's the reason I smile most days." He fiddled with the ornament, double-checked its distance from the other baubles, and then collected his glass. "Another eggnog, anyone?"

Vicky and I nodded, and he gathered our glasses

before disappearing into the kitchen.

"Poor guy," Vicky said, shooting me a look that said I should've kept my mouth shut.

"I know. Hey, do you remember Mrs Simon?"

Vicky pondered this for a moment, sucking on her bottom lip. "Sure. She used to bake those really nice scones and hot cross buns."

"Trust you to remember that."

"What? They were good!"

We shared a smile that made my insides warm. We could be friends if we kept eye contact to a minimum. That might work.

I plucked another piece of silver tinsel and hung it over the mantelpiece, careful not to disturb any pictures of Mabel.

"She also gave out those cool dinosaur plasters, remember? When me, you, and Cameron were trying to build the world's biggest bike jump on the field?"

A memory surfaced in my mind's eye. "Oh, yeah. We thought we were going to break a world record, but I bet in reality it was only about this high." I held my arm to my waist and laughed. Cameron's face lingered in my memory, his spindly arms in the air with his T-shirt tan and a grin too big for his face. But it didn't tear at me like it usually did. It was a warm ache in my chest...but a nice one. It made me feel close to him.

"He always had us doing crazy things, didn't he?"

Vicky said quietly, joining me by the mantelpiece and pretending to look at a picture of Mabel.

"He did, yeah."

"I wonder what he'd think of all this."

A smile tugged at my mouth. "He always thought we would end up together." The words left my mouth without realising. *Shit.* I glanced at her, trying to gauge her reaction.

Vicky kept looking straight ahead. I swear her cheeks were turning pink. "That's not what I meant."

"I know."

Vicky swatted at me, but she smiled too, shaking her head. "You always did know how to push my buttons."

I wondered if I'd be able to do the same in the bedroom. The thought jumped into my head before I could stop it. Then I felt my own cheeks start to redden. *Just friends. Just friends. Just friends.* I put a bit more space between us.

"What's that look for?" Vicky asked.

I turned away just as Mr Simon returned with our second eggnog. *Perfect timing.* I avoided Vicky's inquisitive gaze and instead admired our handiwork about the room. The place had such a Christmassy feel to it now, it almost put me back into a Christmassy mood. Almost.

Vicky's phone rang, and she fished it out of her pocket. She watched the screen for a few moments, her lips pressed together. "I should probably get this."

I watched as she exited the room, something sinking in my chest. Thoughts of tomorrow swirled in my mind. Would Tanya be there? Probably.

Honestly, I wasn't sure I was ready to meet her, ever.

"You okay, my dear?" Mr Simon asked.

I turned my attention to him, forcing a smile on my face, but he wasn't addressing me. It was Mabel, who had strolled into the room with the confidence of a runway model. She let out a little meow at the sight of her owner and tangled herself between his legs.

Mr Simon laughed. I wasn't sure I'd heard him laugh before. At least not in a long time.

"Your friend's here." He plucked her up and cradled her in his arms, stroking her ginger and white fur. Mabel looked at me as if noticing me for the first time, her green eyes studying me with intrigue.

"Hey, Mabel." I tickled behind her white ear, and she pressed into my hand, letting out a soft purr.

"That's her favourite spot. How did you know?"

Cameron and I loved animals. We'd never had a cat, but we'd pretended Mabel was ours when we saw her outside, and often kept little treats in our pockets, just in case. "I remembered. She always liked it before." I noted the grey hairs around her eyes and neck, the way her eyes were slightly clouded. A wave of sadness washed over me. What would Mr Simon do when Mabel was gone?

I swallowed, thinking of him removing all her

pictures and leaving an empty mantelpiece. The ever-present reminder of death skirted around my peripheral vision. Time really did wait for no one.

"I'm gonna head out now," Vicky said, standing in the doorway. "It's been lovely to see you, Mr Simon."

He waved his free hand, balancing Mabel in the other. "Jeff, please. I've known you since you were a baby, Victoria. No need for pleasantries now. But thank you, dear. It's been lovely to see you too."

Vicky nodded, smiling slightly at the use of her full name. "Alright then, Jeff. I'll see you soon." She glanced at me. "Are you coming?"

"I'm gonna stay a while." I turned back to Mr Simon; calling him Jeff felt unnatural to me. "If that's okay with you, of course?"

Mr Simon couldn't hide the surprise on his face. He smiled a toothy grin and nodded a little sheepishly. "You're always welcome here."

Something in Vicky's posture softened as she looked between us. "Okay. I'll see you tomorrow then, Holly?"

I nodded. "I'll be there."

We shared another smile, one that pulled at my insides, and then she was gone.

I sucked in a deep breath, feeling an ache open in her absence. I definitely did not want to start thinking about what that meant right now. I sipped at my eggnog, savouring the sweet taste. "Do you fancy watching a

Christmas film? I bet you have a great collection."

Mr Simon beamed. "I do, actually. We could watch *A Christmas Carol*. It's mine and Mabel's favourite."

I wanted to appeal for a different choice, but if it was Mr Simon's favourite, I'd suck it up. "That sounds great."

He popped in the film and settled in his armchair, Mabel curling up on his lap. I took a seat on the sofa, taking in my surroundings. The fairy lights glowed and dimmed in a steamy rhythm, casting red and silver off the baubles and onto the walls. The opening credits began, and Mr Simon hummed along to the music.

Suddenly, I imagined Cameron sitting beside me. I could almost hear his voice, the sarcastic tone as he'd roll his eyes at watching a film that was pre-2000s, never mind one in black-and-white. I took comfort in the feel of his presence ghosting around me and questioned if Mr Simon allowed the same feeling with his late wife—or if shutting her out meant that wasn't possible. I wondered if putting up her photo would make any difference. Could Cameron's pictures change how I felt too?

I glanced at him, taking in the contemplative look on his face as he combed a hand gently through Mabel's fur.

"Hey, Mr Simon. Do you have any plans for Christmas dinner?"

Chapter
Seventeen

Christmas Eve rolled around, bringing with it the fresh smell of gingerbread as Mum pulled tray after tray out of the oven. I'd come downstairs to investigate after hearing the cupboards banging and swear words being thrown at the dog. Mum's dark hair was tied up in a bun, an apron displaying a man's six-pack wrapped around her waist. We'd bought it as a joke present for Dad a few years ago; the sight of it on her made me smile.

Mum looked up as I entered the kitchen, red-faced and with flour sprinkled up her arms. Butterbee lay at her feet, waiting for any crumbs. "Merry Christmas Eve, love." She flung the oven door shut and shoved the last tray on the counter, wiping her face with her sleeve.

"Merry Christmas Eve, Mum." I dusted the flour off her face with my hand and then pulled her in for a hug.

Mum squeezed me tight, probably getting flour on me, but I didn't mind. When we parted, she eyed me with a hand on her hip. "What was that for?"

I bent down to scratch Butterbee's soft head. "What?"

"The hug. Are you feeling alright? Do you have a temperature?" she joked.

"Give over." Butterbee rolled over, giving me access to full tummy rubs. I happily obliged. "I can give my mother a hug and not be coming down with a fever."

"Well, I suppose so." She smiled, brushed her hands over her apron, and looked at the gingerbread with a small sigh.

I could take a guess what she was thinking. Baking gingerbread had been something we did every Christmas Eve. Cameron and I had an annual competition to see who could decorate the best gingerbread house. It always ended in a unanimous draw, of course; Mum and Dad were always unable to pick a favourite, but that never stopped our competitive behaviour. We'd fallen out one year when we were eight or nine, when Cameron "accidentally" knocked my North Pole masterpiece to the floor. He'd been sent to his room while Mum tried to salvage the broken pieces, but it was a lost cause. Later that evening, Cameron slipped a note under my door, a simple "I'm sorry", along with his favourite shiny Pokémon card. We'd spent the rest of the night listening for reindeer on the roof and drawing pictures of Pokémon to leave as a present for Father Christmas.

"You want help decorating them?" I asked Mum, gesturing to the gingerbread on the side.

Her head snapped to me, her mouth slightly agape. "You…you want to help me decorate?"

"Sure." I gave her a small smile, hoping she wouldn't start crying. I couldn't bear to watch Mum cry. There was something so wrong about it when she was usually so put together.

She pressed her lips together and gave a few swift nods. "That would be nice." Her eyes started to gloss over. I needed to get out of here before the waterworks opened. Had she done this by herself for the past two years? Guilt clawed at my throat, but I tried to swallow it down. Carrying on this tradition clearly meant a lot to her. *I should have been here.*

"Okay. Give me a shout when they're cool." I bolted back down the hallway and up the stairs. This time, I let my gaze browse the pictures: Cameron with his arm around me on sports day; Cameron covered in chocolate ice cream by the beach; me grinning, buried up to my neck in the sand by Cameron and Dad. School pictures. Big toothless smiles and birthday cakes and football games.

All of our lives in 4x5 gloss.

People had always told me we looked alike, but I could see it now. We had the same almond-shaped eyes, brown like Dad's, and soft jawlines and cheekbones. Cameron had a bigger nose and facial hair in the more recent photos, but the similarities were still there.

How much of him did people see when they looked at me? Did Mum and Dad? Vicky too? Was that painful?

I stopped on the top step, struck by one of the last photos. Cameron's brown hair was sticking out of his helmet as he posed at the top of the ski slope. He must've been thirteen or fourteen, all gangly legs and acne. I stared at it for a while, burning his smile into my mind. My heart ached, pulling memories from the recesses. But I let them surface: drinking so much hot chocolate on the ski slopes we nearly peed our pants; playing on inflatables on the river behind our house. So many secrets, and so much laughter it could never be contained. And why should it? It was one of the best times of my life.

My legs were moving before I thought about it, my limbs acting of their own accord as I put my hand on the handle and opened the door to Cameron's room.

I hadn't been in there for years. It was different from how I remembered. Emptier, for one thing, but then it had been over five years since he'd occupied this space. The walls were still the same slate grey, with the double bed in the corner, but his pictures and photos now lay in labelled boxes. *Cameron's stuff.*

How strange to have all our worldly possessions lumped together. Everything that meant something all combined to just *stuff.* I lingered in the doorway, considering whether I had the courage to actually set foot inside.

Yes, Holly. You can do this.

I moved a step forward. The smell was muted, but it was still him. I couldn't understand how that was possible. Before I could change my mind, I dropped to my knees and opened the first box. I thumbed over school reports, pencil drawings, and old, cheap medals from various sports events over the years. I opened another, finding stacks and stacks of photos. I sifted through them, smiling at one of the two of us and Vicky with ice creams in our hands.

A few loose tears fell down my cheeks. I wiped them on my sleeve, determined to keep going. I didn't want to end up like Mr Simon.

I didn't want to run any more.

I put the picture to one side and shuffled through the others, laughing at one where the three of us were dressed up as Smurfs. Cameron was waving some sweets at the camera, his tongue out and stained red. Vicky had her arm around my shoulder. She'd always been there for me. Had I been there for her? If I'd coped with his death differently, would things between us be different too?

There was no point getting hung up on things I couldn't change. But I could try to be better going forward.

I got lost in the boxes, caught in a mix of smiles and laughter and tears as the memories bombarded me. I separated some pictures into my own pile, planning to put them up when I got back home. It struck me as odd, not for the first time this week, to think of London as my home. Everything seemed spun on its head. The more time I spent here, the less I felt like going back to my apartment and the life that I had there.

My gaze caught on a handmade photo frame covered in painted pasta and glitter. It must have been one of Cameron's design projects at school. I flipped it over and let out a breath. *Best friends forever* was written across the top of the frame in colourful pipe cleaners. Slotted in little cut-outs was a collage of photos of me, Vicky, and Cameron, no older than ten years old. I took my time looking over each picture. Stained from time or the sun, most were faded or discoloured, but the sentiment was there, squeezing something in my chest.

Mum called up to me, announcing that the gingerbread was cool enough to start decorating. I sighed, unable to tear my eyes from the picture frame. The messy glue stains and the wonky letter placement, all so imperfectly Cameron. He'd never had the patience for creative stuff like that. He was always much more the "get up and get 'em" type of guy. I think without his encouragement, I might've fallen into the background. He gave me the confidence to try new things, to build the big bike ramps and to jump off the highest rope-swings. He comforted me when I needed it, and called me out when I didn't. He was the first person I told about my feelings for Vicky. And he was the first person to tell me to do something about it.

Granted, I didn't always take his advice. I hoped he wouldn't be disappointed with the way I'd been after his death.

"I'm still learning, Cam," I murmured. "And I still miss you every day."

I placed the photo frame onto my selected pile and headed downstairs with the photos in my arms.

Mum was rattling around the kitchen, even though we still had hours until we were due at the Castletons' for Christmas Eve dinner. I could hear Dad watching a Christmas-themed gameshow in the living room. The freshly baked gingerbread made me salivate.

"The gingerbread assembly team has arrived." I looked over the different shapes: Christmas trees, Santas, snowmen, and little reindeer. "No gingerbread houses this year?"

Mum clumsily poured the icing into the blue pipette bag, squeezing it down towards the bottom of the tube. "No...I...haven't done those in a while."

I nodded, able to read between the lines. "No worries. We can try some next year maybe."

She glanced at me. "Really? You'll come back up next year?"

"Yeah. But I'll definitely be back up before then, Mum."

She pouted her lip, and her eyes watered again. *Oh, no, please don't cry.* She turned her attention to the piping bag and asked, "What've you got there, love?"

"Oh, I've been looking through some of Cameron's stuff, and I wanted to check with you before I take these?"

"You've been looking through Cameron's things?" Mum didn't even try to hide her emotions this time, they were written all over her face. Disbelief, surprise, relief.

I hesitated, knocked momentarily by my own swirl of feelings. "I have. I'd like to put up some more pictures. To…talk about him more."

"That's great, love. Really great." Mum smiled, a stray tear rolling down her cheek. She brushed it with the back of her hand, streaking black mascara across her face.

"Here, Mum. You're going to look like one of those emus."

She let out a chuckle, and I wiped the marks away. She looked like she wanted to say something else, but instead, she picked up the piping bag and passed it to me.

I steadied my hand over the first gingerbread Christmas tree. "So you're sure you're okay with me taking these photos?"

Mum nodded, peering over my shoulder. "Okay with me. I'm happy to see you aren't shutting him out any more. I was worried about you."

I swallowed, making a big wobble in the tinsel icing. A few beats passed before I had the courage to speak. "I'm sorry for not coming back sooner, Mum."

Neither of us said anything for a moment. The Christmas gameshow filtered in through the walls, along with Dad shouting, "It's Ebenezer Scrooge, you bloody idiot!"

Mum placed her head on my shoulder, and I relaxed at the touch. "I'm just happy you're with us now, love." Warmth spread through my chest, and true happiness extended to the tips of my fingers. "Now, chop chop. Let's make this the best gingerbread the Castletons have ever seen."

Chapter Eighteen

Standing on the Castletons' front step with a gigantic box of gingerbread in my hands, I was the most nervous I'd been in years. Mum had made Dad dress in his navy blue Christmas shirt, which sported cartoon Christmas trees and Santa hats.

He linked his arm in mine, his aftershave burning my nostrils. He always put on three sprays too many.

Mum turned to flash me an encouraging smile. She'd straightened her dark hair for the occasion and was wearing a tasteful red dress that perfectly matched her lipstick and hugged her figure. She'd been extra nice to me ever since the mix-up with Vicky and our heart-to-heart earlier. I felt some reassurance from her.

If I can go into Cameron's room and look through his

photos, I can do a Christmas Eve dinner with the Castletons.

And Tanya Jones.

The door flung open. Vicky's mum Denise greeted us with a huge smile, waving us in off the doorstep. Their hallway already smelled like garlic and rosemary, and my belly gurgled at the thought. Denise was a good cook— unlike Mum, who always ended up in a bit of a tangle with most of the ingredients on herself or the floor. But at least Butterbee had a good time.

"Would you like any drinks? Fizz? Wine? Beer?" Denise fussed, guiding us into the living room where their dining table had been extended to accommodate the extra guests. A big Christmas tree stood in the corner, covered in golden beads and tinsel. Vicky's dad, Jim, greeted us with a big hug before flying into the kitchen at Denise's request to get the drinks.

Music played quietly from a Christmas best hits channel on the TV, and standing beside it was Vicky and the very long legs of Tanya Jones.

A hot rod stabbed my chest, contorting and twisting it. I couldn't look away from the slender arm wrapped around Vicky's shoulder—or the shoulder-length auburn hair and the striped Armani dress hugging her perfect figure. I forced a smile, hoping it came across as friendly and not constipated, and Vicky began the mountain of introductions.

Tanya gave everyone a hug and a kiss on the cheek, and I tried not to recoil at the touch. *Where is Jim with that damn drink?*

I avoided looking directly at Vicky, and instead found renewed interest in the knitted ornaments hanging on the tree—Denise's doing, I imagined. Jim brought in our glasses of prosecco, and the festivities could begin. I sipped at my fizz, putting so much energy into forced smiling I didn't realise I was being directly addressed.

Mum nudged me and nodded at Denise, who was watching me expectantly.

"I'm sorry. Did you say something?"

"I said it's so lovely to see you again, Holly. We've missed having you around." She smiled at me so genuinely that I had no choice but to believe her. She had the same blue eyes as Vicky—eyes that seemed to look and really see, in a way that made it difficult to look at her right now for fear of being exposed.

I forced another smile. "It's been nice to be back." *For the most part.*

"And thanks for helping out so much with the business while I've had to work."

"No problem. It's been fun." I felt Vicky's gaze on me, but I couldn't meet it. This was much harder than I'd thought it would be. Which meant I cared much more than I wanted to admit. *Dammit.*

"Sit down, everyone. I hope you're hungry." Denise

dragged Jim into the kitchen while the rest of us took our places. I was seated next to Mum, opposite Vicky. It wasn't the worst placement in the world, but it meant I'd have to keep my eyes down on my plate if I had any hope of surviving the evening with my heart still intact. *Why did I agree to stay until New Year? Why, why, why?*

Would Mum understand if I told her I needed to leave early? The happiness on her face when I'd helped her make the gingerbread flashed in my mind's eye. We'd just started healing. I probably shouldn't start poking old wounds. Plus, it would negate my resolution to stop running from things...though, technically, it wasn't the New Year yet.

The wise choice would be to distance myself from Vicky until the resurfaced feelings quelled themselves. I wished Cameron were here. He'd know what to do.

Denise and Jim brought in plates of steaming finger foods: sausage rolls, mini quiches, and pigs in blankets, with dishes of roasted vegetables in butter and herbs. A selection of meats and cheeses claimed the centrepiece, and the aroma of everything almost made me forget my inner turmoil.

"Dig in," Denise said, waving her arms in encouragement.

Dad wasted no time in piling the crispy potatoes onto his plate, followed by a handful of pigs in blankets. Mum tutted him but picked up a small quiche, and the rest of us followed suit. It was much easier to pretend I was okay when I had something to occupy myself with. And the fact that it was delicious made all of it easier to swallow.

"So…Tanya," Mum began, pausing for effect. "I've not seen you before. Are you from around here?"

Tanya looked up from her teeny tiny plate consisting of just olives and fluttered her long eyelashes. "I'm not from here, no, but my dad has some business in the area. I'm from Cambridge originally."

Mum nodded while I continued to shove potatoes in my mouth. "Interesting. And what business might that be?"

"The new housing estate being built on the fields here, among other things." She popped an olive in her mouth and chewed slowly.

"I see. So it's your family that's responsible for a lot of the expansions around here. The queues at the Co-op are longer than I've ever known."

Trust Mum to be irked about the check-out queues.

"There's a lot of room for growth. Dad's working on it. The place has a lot of potential." Tanya beamed at Mum, but she wasn't having any of it.

"Have you tried the pigs in blankets, Alan?" Jim asked.

Dad nodded, his mouth full of something. It was a good attempt at a conversation pivot, but not good enough.

"And how did you and our Vicky meet?" Mum asked, giving Tanya the third degree.

"Mum," I hissed.

"What?" She feigned innocence. "I'm just being polite."

Just being nosy more like.

Tanya let out a soft laugh. "It's no problem. It's only human nature to be inquisitive."

So Tanya thinks Mum is nosy too. I guess we have something in common.

Her brown eyes met mine before resting on Mum. "Vicky and I met online, actually. It's so much easier than trying to meet organically."

"Well...that sounds nice." Mum took a little sip of her prosecco while Cliff Richard filled the silence from the TV.

Yes, so very "nice". Like a nice bit of open-heart surgery or a nice trip to the dentist for some teeth-pulling.

Denise and Jim took a swig from their drinks, sharing a wordless glance. *Someone, please say something else.*

"I usually travel a lot, so it is rather nice to be back for Christmas," Tanya continued. "And Mistleberry is so cute. What about you?"

It took a moment for me to look up from my plate. "Me?"

She gave a tight smile. "How did you and Vicky meet?"

"Oh, erm, well, we've known each other as long as I can remember."

"That's interesting." Tanya popped another olive in her mouth. Judging by her tone, it was anything *but* interesting.

"There's only a couple of months between them," Denise added. "Inseparable since they were babies."

"Ah, yes. It's your little childhood friend, isn't it?" Tanya directed at Vicky.

Little? There was nothing about me that was little. It was just that she was abnormally tall. I retreated into my glass, guzzling the prosecco. A strained silence fell over the table as knives and forks scraped plates. I caught Denise's eye, and she gave me a gentle smile.

Oh, god. Is that pity? Did Denise and Jim know about my feelings for Vicky? Did Tanya?

I shoved another tiny quiche in my mouth, hoping no one would ask me any further questions.

The dinner topic switched to Denise's business and her plans for the future. Her current hours working at the care home limited production; she hoped to get a small team together so they could produce more once she retired. I wondered if Vicky had expressed her hope of getting involved and taking it to the next level.

With a little prompt from me, Mum gushed over Biscuit and her love for horses. Vicky joined in with her love for Crystal, and Dad and I shared a knowing look.

Once Mum got started talking about horses, you couldn't get a word in edgeways—unless it was to discuss marriage or potential grandbabies. I was just happy the conversation was off me for a change.

Jim cleared the plates while Denise brought in the dessert: hot apple pie and custard, and a chocolate Yule log with cream and chocolate shavings. Tanya insisted she couldn't eat any more, and with the amount of carbs I'd been eating since I'd been home (probably half my weight in custard creams), I should've declined too. But something in me protested as soon as the words left her mouth. I didn't want to be lumped in the same group as her. The unfun dessert-decliners.

I opted for the Yule log, and its soft creamy chocolatey goodness didn't disappoint.

"Wow, Denise. I don't know how we're going to eat a thing tomorrow." I leaned back in my chair, my belly pushing against the buttons on my jeans.

Vicky's hand caught my attention, and she smiled and pointed at her mouth.

"You've got a chocolate moustache," she mouthed.

"Oh." I picked up my napkin and wiped my face, catching Vicky's smile. Tanya must have seen something too, as she glanced between us.

"It was absolutely beautiful, Denise. You've outdone yourself." Dad let out a little sigh of contentment and sipped from his glass.

Jim wiped his beard with a napkin and raised his own.

Vicky groaned. "Oh, no, Dad, no toasts tonight, please." She hung her head, and her mother tapped her playfully.

"Don't be like that, Vicky, it's Christmas. Go ahead, Jim."

"To my darling wife, for putting on this wonderful spread." He kissed her hand, and she giggled, shooing him away. "And to great friends, old and new. I'm very grateful for your friendship over the years. I'll not embarrass you with a kiss, Alan, but I'll blow you one instead." Dad made a show of catching the kiss and tucking it into his pocket. "I'm so proud of my *amazing* daughter. You've worked so hard at university, and I know it's all gonna pay off for you."

Vicky shook her head, but she smiled. "Thanks, Dad."

Jim blew her a kiss too, then turned his attention to Tanya. "Tanya, I hope you've enjoyed your first Christmas Eve with us. It's been lovely to spend a bit of time with you when you're not gallivanting all over the globe. Our Vicky is a lucky lady."

"Dad." Vicky groaned again. I echoed the sentiment.

The fizz had glazed Jim's eyes, and his cheeks were tinted red. Undeterred, he ignored Vicky and looked at me.

Oh, god. I gripped my glass tighter, nervous about what was going to come out of his mouth next.

"And, Holly, in many ways, you're like a second daughter to me. I can't imagine what it was like to lose your brother like that, but we'll keep him alive in our memories. Like the time he gifted me that lovely toilet brush one year and said it reminded him of my beard." We all laughed, and he grinned at the memory. "Anyway, it warms my heart to see you doing better. Welcome home." He reached his glass into the middle of the table for a cheers. "Merry Christmas, everyone. We love you, Cameron."

We clinked our glasses and echoed his toast. Mum was close to tears, and Vicky's gaze had softened. A familiar warmth flushed through my chest at being around these people who meant so much to me. Something gripped my heart and squeezed hard. I felt my own eyes pricking. But I wasn't about to cry in front of Tanya.

Vicky's attention flickered to me, something unexplainable moving between us. As though she could sense how I was feeling. She smiled softly, and the squeezing loosened, letting me breathe easily again.

Tanya clinked her glass, and everyone turned to her. "That was very touching, Jim. I just want to add a few words."

She was addressing Vicky, and my heart plummeted to my feet. Whatever was about to follow was going to hurt like hell.

"These three months with you have truly been the best of my life," Tanya said. "I'm tremendously excited to see where our business venture will lead us, and to get to travel the world with you."

Business venture? Travel the world?

Mum and I exchanged curt glances. I'd thought Vicky was considering working with Pertoni Clark, or else starting her mum's business plan. The warmth I'd felt in my chest earlier chilled and cracked, sending splinters into my sides. I swallowed. I'd finally reconciled with Vicky and realised my feelings for her and what I wanted. I'd been trying to find a way to keep her in my life, but it was slipping away. I could see it. I could feel it in my veins.

Tanya took Vicky's hand and gazed at her longingly. My breath stuck in my throat. *Is she going to fucking propose?*

I couldn't look. I stared down at my empty plate, feeling the chocolate goodness in my stomach start to curdle and churn. *Don't do this here. Not now.*

"So much is going splendidly for us, but we're not stopping there. My dad has organised a new apartment beside the Thames for me. So Vicky and I are going to move in together."

Oh. Oh. *Oh.*

Fifty different emotions battled it out in my head.

Relief, followed by hurt, and then disappointment. I sucked a deep breath in and squashed them all down, leaving a dull ache that pushed me into my chair. I still couldn't look. It wasn't a marriage proposal, but it was a definite end. Did they really have to move to fucking London? The city? It was the one place I had to escape them. And I thought Vicky didn't want to move to the city, anyway?

I wanted to be closer to Vicky, but not like this.

Not like this.

As the congratulations rang out, I forced a smile on my face, letting the familiar ache consume me, dragging me further into the ground beneath my seat. As the voices joined together, swirling into nothingness, I imagined Cameron sitting beside me, tutting and shaking his head.

Too late, Holly. Too little, too late.

Chapter Nineteen

Christmas at the Bradfields' always had a few certainties.
One: Dad would get too drunk. Two: Mum would burn
something in the oven. Three: by the end of the night,
we'd gather around the telly and watch something
Christmassy, our bellies full and our faces hurting from
smiling.

Cameron, of course, had been a huge part of
Christmas. These past two Christmases I hadn't been able
to bear the thought of staring at his empty place at the
table, or having to put up with Mum's moaning over the
turkey and Dad's terrible jokes on my own. Working
overtime in the office had been the perfect distraction—
except it didn't distract me at all. I still spent Christmas
thinking about Cameron, crying into the computer

keyboard and thinking about my parents celebrating the holiday without me. I hated myself for it.

This year, I couldn't think of anywhere else I'd rather be. Christmas had its certainties, that was true, but it also had its wild cards. Like Mr Simon joining us for Christmas dinner, and Vicky Castleton declaring her plans to move in with her girlfriend.

But we're not focusing on that last one.

Mum burned the roast carrots, blaming Nigella for her faulty recipe after she'd insisted on making them when she was three sherries in. But apart from that, the dinner was a success. We ate almost everything, which was impressive considering we'd cooked extra "just in case", and settled around the table wearing our multi-coloured Christmas paper hats. We'd lit a candle for Cameron, which flickered away on the mantelpiece next to a family photo. The flame danced in the baubles on the Christmas tree, drawing me in with its magnetising glow.

We'd all had our individual moments today when it felt like our worlds were falling apart. Mine came in the early hours of the morning, remembering how Cameron and I would bolt into our parents' room and jump on their bed. Mum would grumble, but Dad would leap up with us, invigorated by the magic of the day. He'd be ready with his camera, taking pictures of us every moment. Cameron and I would race down the stairs, pushing and shoving to be the first to open the door and look under the

Christmas tree to see if the big man had been.

Walking down the stairs this morning, the memories bombarded me, stuffing me so full with feelings I felt I might burst. Cameron's presence had ghosted by me most of the day, and along with the sadness, the sensation left me feeling tingly and warm. I'd felt closer to him this week than I had for two years. I guess sometimes walking headfirst into that pain was the best way to deal with it. The Buck's Fizz helped too.

I tore my attention away from the candle and zoned in on the conversation. Dad and Mr Simon were discussing their favourite Simon & Garfunkel songs, both getting animated with their hands. Jeff insisted that the duo's chilling rendition of "Silent Night" was one of their best works, whereas Dad claimed nothing would ever beat "The Sound of Silence". Mum caught my gaze and rolled her eyes, but she was smiling. It was nice for things to feel light and easy. Surprisingly, it had been a relaxed Christmas, but that didn't stop my mind from wandering.

Had Vicky and Tanya spent the day together? Most likely. What had Tanya bought her? Probably something expensive.

I sighed. I hadn't had the chance to give Vicky her present yesterday. It just never seemed like the right moment. I didn't know whether to leave it altogether.

Mr Simon stood, patting his belly, which was now poking over his belt. "I must say, that's the best dinner

I've had since Judy passed away. Thank you for your hospitality, but I'd better be off. I don't want to leave Mabel on her own for too long." He made a point of looking at each of us in turn. "Thank you."

He held out his hand, but Dad stood and batted it away, pulling him in for a hug. Mr Simon had clearly not had as much to drink as Dad; he stood there a little awkwardly while Dad slapped him affectionately on the back.

"You come around any time, Jeff."

"Thank you," he mumbled. "We will sort out a day to listen to those tracks too, on the ol' turntable."

"Definitely."

They separated, and Dad wobbled his way to the kitchen, probably to get another beer. Mr Simon turned to me and patted down his pockets. He pulled out a boiled sweet, a small collection of change, and then a white envelope. He brushed the envelope off and handed it to me.

"Mr Simon—"

He held up his palms. "Now, now. It's just a little something to say thank you for all your help before. Please, just take it."

I slipped a finger under the seal and shimmied it open, half-expecting to find a snippet of Mabel's hair in there. Instead, I pulled out two tickets.

"The Donnington Ice Fair," I read aloud.

"I'm not in the loop with all you young folk now, but Betty down at the shop said this was going to be a great event." He smiled a little sheepishly. "Of course, you don't have to go if you don't want to."

"No, this sounds like fun." Though I didn't know what exactly an ice fair consisted of, Donnington was only a few towns over. It was known for its expensive properties and housed a few low-level celebrities too. The tickets probably cost a lot of money.

"Would you like to take the extra ticket?" I asked him. "We could make a day of it."

He drew his bushy brows together. "Oh, no, that ticket is for Victoria."

Oh. That realisation made everything else fly right out of my head. I was very unsure of our situation at the moment. I didn't know if it was the best idea to spend time with her. I needed to start distancing myself. I was leaving soon anyway, and Vicky was moving on with her life. I should do the same.

Mr Simon's gaze burned into me, awaiting his answer, so I nodded. "That's very sweet of you, Jeff. Thank you." I put the tickets on the table and gave him a smile. A lightbulb went off in my head. "I actually got you a little something too." I ran upstairs, plucked the photo of Cameron and me with Mabel off my dresser and slotted it into an envelope. I returned to the living room and handed it to him.

He raised a wild brow at me as he delicately opened it and slid the picture out.

"I found this and thought it might make a good addition to your mantelpiece. I told you, Mabel and I have been friends for a long time. I think Cam would've liked you to have it too. So Mabel won't forget him."

He stared at the picture for a while before glancing up at me. Then he swallowed, blinking rapidly. "It's lovely. Very thoughtful. I know just the place for it." He sniffed and shook his head. "Anyhoo…I'd better be off. Thank you again. Both of you." He nodded and headed into the hallway to put on his shoes and coat, leaving Mum and me alone at the table with Butterbee under our feet.

"What are you gonna do?"

I looked away from the door to find Mum watching me intently, one hand around her wineglass. She gestured towards the tickets on the table.

"I'm not sure." I exhaled and reached for my own glass, but it was already empty. The day's events were starting to weigh on me. Now that Christmas was mostly over, reality was beginning to set in. New Year's Eve was just a week away, and afterwards, I'd be going back home. But home and London didn't seem to be synonymous any more. Just like the beginning of last week, I felt out of place again. I hadn't realised just how much I'd missed Mistleberry.

"Jeff," Dad said from inside the kitchen, "who is Father Christmas's favourite singer?"

"Not another one, Alan," Mr Simon grumbled from the hall.

Mum and I exchanged glances, smiling and rolling our eyes.

"Elfis Presley." Dad broke out laughing, and then the door opened, and Mr Simon poked his head through.

"Just saying goodbye. Thanks again, and Merry Christmas!"

"Merry Christmas, Jeff!" we echoed.

Dad stumbled back into the living room with a fresh pint in his hand and took his favourite chair over by the window. He'd be asleep in less than five minutes. I'd guarantee it.

He turned on the TV and flicked through a few channels. "Tracy, *Home Alone* is on!"

"We'll be over in a minute." Mum tapped her nails on the table, drawing my attention to her. The silver necklace I'd bought her for Christmas shone under the brass light fitting. "I've gone the whole day without saying something, love. But enough is enough."

My mouth fell open. But before I could say anything else, she continued, "You've got to speak to Vicky."

I groaned. "Mum—"

"Don't 'Mum' me. I'm serious. Are you going to let her get away?"

"Mum. There's nothing to get away from."

She furrowed her eyebrows.

"You know what I mean. Nothing's happened between us. She's got her own life. She's got a girlfriend, for god's sake."

"So you're telling me what I saw in your bedroom was nothing?" Mum pressed her lips together.

"Pfft. You didn't see anything."

"Holly Alexandra Bradfield."

I startled at the use of my full name. Mum never used it unless I was in big trouble.

She slapped her hand on the table, then balled it into a fist. "I may not be the smartest woman, the best chef, or able to knit any of those goddamn knitting patterns Denise sent me," she went on. "I don't know a lot of things, but I know about love." Her gaze softened, and she relaxed her hand flat against the wood. "When two people look at each other the way you two do…that's not just 'nothing'. It's quite the opposite."

I looked down at my lap. Heat flushed my cheeks as I remembered how safe and warm I'd felt in Vicky's arms. How good it felt to close the space between us. The way my heart raced whenever I saw her. Mum had a point, but that didn't change anything. She had a girlfriend. I wasn't getting involved.

I sighed, playing with the rim of my empty glass. "She's got a different life, Mum. *She's* different. She's got plans, and she has…Tanya."

"All I know is the way that girl speaks about you, it's like you're the bloody North Star." She shook her head, jiggling her long gold earrings. She was about to say something else but paused, pressing her lips together. Then she started again in a small voice. "And when you weren't here, love, she always asked after you. She missed you—we all did, but she always said you'd come back when you were ready. She never stopped talking about you, you know."

Guilt nibbled at my insides. Vicky had been such a good friend to me, despite all the mistakes of my past. She still believed in me, still wanted to try, even now. Just because she was in a relationship didn't mean I should throw all that away. I needed to try as well. Even if it wasn't the way I wanted it to be, our friendship was worth it. Could I really just run away again?

Both of us were silent for a minute. The TV filled the quiet, and I glanced at the screen to see Kevin setting up traps to catch the burglars. Cameron had loved this film too. I smiled softly and turned back to Mum, but she was still deep in thought, tracing patterns in the wood with her fingertips.

She looked up, snaring me with her brown eyes. "I don't know if there's ever a reason for the terrible things that happen, Holly. We know that more than anyone." She looked to the candle briefly, watching the flames flicker and dance. "But some things transcend all of those complications. I see it in the two of you when you're together. One of those unexplainable things…it binds you two together. Fight for it, love. Don't waste it."

The weight of everything pressed on my chest. I'd never felt about anyone the way I'd felt about Vicky. Whenever I was with her, I felt whole, like another part of me had finally found its way home. But…it was complicated. I'd never been in these shoes, never had to watch her be with someone else…not like she had with me.

I cursed myself. I was being selfish. Again. I needed to be there for Vicky, to make up for my misdoings in the past. Mum was right, Vicky was special. I needed her in my life, even if it hurt.

"Bloody hell," Dad called from his armchair. "Since when did you start talking like Mystic Meg, Trace?"

"Shut up, Alan." Mum rolled her eyes and then refilled our glasses with the last of the prosecco. She raised her glass to mine, her eyes sparkling with that knowing look of hers. "So, what will it be, love?"

"What happened to Santa when he went speed-dating?" Dad asked with a slight slur to his words.

"Alan!" Mum blew out a breath. "This is serious. Our daughter's happiness hangs in the balance."

Boy, what a way to phrase it, Mum.

"Aw, come on, Trace. I'm not going to be able to tell

any more Christmas jokes tomorrow."

Mum took a big gulp from her prosecco.

"Go on, Dad," I said. "What happened to Santa when he went speed-dating?"

He sat up in his chair, grinning wildly. "He pulled a cracker."

A little laugh escaped me. Okay, that one was pretty good. Not that I'd ever admit that, though. Even Mum failed to hide her smile.

I gripped my glass and caught Mum's eye. Her eyebrows quirked with anticipation. I let her hang for a moment, then I grinned, trying to contain my laughter. "You know what they say. There's snow time like the present."

"Jesus Christ." Her eyes narrowed, and she retreated into her prosecco once more.

Dad belly-laughed, slapping his hands on his knees. "That's my daughter, alright. This is Claus for a celebration!"

Mum groaned. "Alan, no, please. That's enough. No more or I'll go to bed!" She shook her head, but her eyes were sparkling.

This was the year to face my fears head-on. I'd done it already, coming home and looking through Cameron's photos. I'd survived that. I could survive this crush on Vicky Castleton too.

But first, I wanted to spend more time with my family. There were at least two more puns I could think of to annoy my mother. That was what Christmas was truly all about.

Chapter Twenty

I was getting a major sense of déjà vu as I waited on the Castletons' step. Every time I found myself back here, I was a bundle of nerves. The temperature had dropped, but I didn't feel the cold so much—probably the wall of defence a day of drinking prosecco will give you.

Mum's words had struck a chord with me. I had a week left here to try to make things right, and if I couldn't, then that was fine. I could live with that. But I was done running. I didn't want to be left with any more regrets. I admired the mix of flashing lights on the street, feeling the glow root somewhere in my heart. It might sound corny, but it felt like hope.

God, how much have I had to drink?

The door swung open, and the glow warming my

chest was extinguished.

Tanya Jones posed in the doorway, her auburn hair perfectly straightened and styled over her shoulders. A pink cashmere jumper clung to her petite figure, black jeans shaping her long, slender legs.

"What a surprise." She smiled a mouth of pearly white teeth and turned to call behind her. "Vikvik, your little friend is here!"

Vikvik? Little friend? I don't know which is worse.

Tanya spun back to face me, her attentive eyes flicking up and down my outfit. Surely she would appreciate my satin Gucci shirt. Her mouth twitched, telling me she did.

"You like fashion?" she asked. "I had one of these. From a few seasons ago, right?"

Well, that doesn't feel like a compliment.

"I'm not sure, I don't keep up with the latest trends as much as I could."

Footsteps down the hallway drew my attention, and Vicky popped up beside Tanya, that beautiful smile of hers instantly making me feel more at ease.

"Holly! Hey, Merry Christmas." Vicky pulled me into a hug, and I gripped her tightly, breathing in her familiar smell.

"Merry Christmas, Vicky," I mumbled into her shoulder.

Another pair of arms found themselves around us.

"Yes, happy Christmas!"

I resisted the urge to roll my eyes. The gift in my hand pressed against someone and rustled. I pulled back, checking it over. The frame was delicate. I really hoped nothing had got squished.

"Oh, I'm sorry," Tanya said. "Is it alright?"

"No worries. It's all good." I forced a smile I didn't really feel and looked down at the gift in my hand, gently pulling at the shiny paper. I didn't really want to do this in front of Tanya, but she hovered, her brown eyes questioning.

At least Vicky could take a hint. "Hey, Tanya, would you mind giving us a minute?"

"No problem." Tanya's eyebrows narrowed slightly as she addressed me. "Nice to see you again."

"Likewise," I replied coolly. After Tanya disappeared down the hallway, I turned to Vicky.

She gave me a look, trying to hide her smile.

"What?"

"Likewise?" She raised an eyebrow. A soft laugh escaped her lips. "What is that all about?"

"I don't know what you mean."

She snorted. "Yeah, right. Anyway, do you want to come in?"

"Oh, no. I've got to get back for the film."

"Which one?"

"*Home Alone*."

"Very nice." She bobbed her head. "A true classic. One of Cam's favourites, right?"

Vicky didn't forget much—sometimes that scared me. She remembered most things about our childhood, and I knew I hadn't always been a shining example of a good friend. But I was trying. "It was, yeah."

"And that Christmas Barbie film he used to make us watch?"

A memory jumped into my brain, and I laughed. "Oh, yeah. I don't know why he liked that so much. I always found that dragon a bit creepy."

"Yeah, well, you used to get scared at everything, so it hardly surprises me."

"Shut up." I jabbed her playfully, and we shared a smile. A cold breeze fluttered around us, drawing us closer together. "Anyway...I got you a little something. Merry Christmas." I handed the gift over to her, feeling suddenly shy. "I'm sorry I didn't give it to you yesterday, but...well..."

"It was a bit weird?" she guessed.

I exhaled, my breath contorting in the cool air. "Yeah. It was a bit weird."

"Holly, about yesterday—"

"Vicky. Not today. It's Christmas! Just open the damn gift before I take it back."

She rolled her eyes, but a smile tugged at her mouth. "Always one for dramatics."

She ripped open the paper messily, studying the package with curious blue eyes. As she slid the frame out of the paper, a handful of emotions rolled across her features. Glancing at me and then back at the frame, she ran her fingers over it carefully, like it might break at any minute.

"Cameron made it. I wanted you to have it."

"I can't accept this, Hol," she said, still looking down at it.

"What, 'cos it's so terrible?"

She let out a breath of laughter. "No. I mean…it's not his best work, but look at us." She angled the frame to me. The three of us posed in a collection of photos, a little faded and worn, but immortalised in time. My heart squeezed, remembering the fun we had together. "Best friends forever," she said quietly, tracing her fingers over the wobbly pipe-cleaners. She shook her head and tried to give it back. "I can't accept this."

"Yes, you can."

Tears flooded Vicky's eyes, and she blinked rapidly, trying to keep them in. "You should keep it."

I placed my hand over hers. "I want you to have it." Her hand felt cold, but I squeezed her fingers. "I wasn't here for you. I broke my promise." I nodded to the *Best friends forever* stuck across the top, and she pressed her lips together. Her lip wobbled. "It wasn't just me that lost a brother," I went on. "You deserve a piece of him too,

Vicky. Please, take it."

A tear slipped down her cheek, and without thinking, I reached out to brush it away. The air stilled between us. Our eyes locked together, and suddenly all I could see was her. That warm silky feeling tangled in my gut, making me feel like I was fifteen again. All I wanted to do was reach out and kiss her, but I retracted my hand, pushing all the gooeyness down.

"Thank you," she said softly.

"You're welcome."

Her eyes found mine again, piercing through my chest and into my heart. Did she always have this way of beguiling me? I'd always assumed it was my doing. Now it was my turn to look away.

With my hands back by my sides, the scene around us started to fade back in: the neighbour's lights flashing, voices and the TV inside, the cool breeze blowing against my face.

"I got you a little something too," Vicky said. "I'll just be one minute." She paused at the door, spinning back to me with the frame held gently to her chest. Her cheeks were tinged pink. "Thank you for this, Hol. I really love it."

She disappeared into the house and left me alone with the darkened sky. Her reaction had twisted something deep inside. I wondered how well she'd coped with Cameron's death. She'd mentioned seeing a counsellor, and that looking after Crystal had helped, but I wish I'd also been there for her.

I sighed, watching my breath dance away into nothingness. Vicky flung open the door again, a small present with reindeer wrapping paper tucked under her arm. She grinned and skipped towards me. Clearly whatever this was had got her excited—and that made me suspicious.

"Is it going to detonate?" I asked.

She rolled her eyes. "No, but that's a good idea for next year. Or your birthday, maybe."

"Charming."

She handed the package to me. It was soft and squishy between my fingers. I gave it a little shake.

"Just open it already!"

I plucked open the sticky tape and folded my finger underneath, shimmying the squidgy ball out of the paper. I pulled it out and burst into laughter. A stuffed knitted cow smiled back at me, its eyes slightly wonky and its big red mouth askew. It was like the design Vicky had sewn onto the ugly tote bag, but it now had a life of its own.

"Oh, my god. I love it! Did you make this?"

"Of course I did. Can't you tell?"

I ran my fingers over the wonky craftsmanship. "Yes, I can actually."

She swatted me, and I dodged out of the way.

"Looks like you and Cameron had the same artistic

talent."

"That doesn't sound like a compliment."

"That's because it isn't."

We burst out laughing, the sound lifting all the weight from my shoulders.

"But really, I love it. I'll treasure it with all my heart."

A smile pulled at her mouth, her blue eyes twinkling. "Good. You better."

The moment stilled again, the air between us sizzling with that unknown something. The unexplainable bond that ties us together. I should probably head back before my heart got carried away.

"Do you have any plans for New Year?" Vicky asked suddenly.

"Well, I guess I'll be going home."

"Right. Of course." Her brows knitted together. "What about the eve? The big countdown?"

"No plans as of yet. Not sure if Mum has anything planned."

"Tanya's family are hosting a party in the great hall by the river, if you fancy it? Should be fun. They're hiring some bands and there will be food and stuff too."

A night watching the two of them together, eating and drinking and dancing and kissing? I wanted to be a good friend to her, but even I knew my limits.

I looked down, folding my hands. "I don't know,

Vicky. I don't know if that's such a good idea."

"Okay. Yeah. Of course. I shouldn't have asked. I'm sorry. I—"

I squeezed her shoulder, and her eyes searched mine. "It's okay. Don't worry about it." I dropped my hand. "Anyway, I'd better be off. If I miss the ending, Mum'll never let me hear the end of it."

Vicky bobbed her head. "Okay. Sure. Thanks again for my present."

"And thanks for mine. I love him." I gave the wonky cow a loving squeeze, earning a smile from her. A thought shot into my head. "Oh, actually. I have these too. Mr Simon gave us them earlier. Two tickets for the Ice Fair at Donnington. I don't really know what it is…but, if you want to go, you can have them. You can take Tanya, if you want."

"That's a sweet offer, but as they're gifts for us, I think we should honour that, don't you?" Vicky eyed the tickets, smiling. "Besides, I should make the most of the time we have."

My tight shoulders fell in relief. For a moment, I thought she was going to turn them down. I'd had mixed feelings about it, but she had a point, our time was limited. Might as well make the most of the time we had left.

"Okay. Cool." Nervous energy rushed through me as the words left my lips. *Ugh. I hate feeling like a teenager.* I loved and hated how out of control my emotions made me feel.

"Merry Christmas, Vicky."

Her eyes met mine, and renewed hope surged through my veins. "Merry Christmas, Holly."

Chapter Twenty-One

With Dad back at work, after the holidays, the house was quieter. I'd managed to get out of horse-shit shovelling duty with Mum, only for the sole reason that I was heading to the Donnington Ice Fair with Vicky.

My phone vibrated on my desk, and Dani's name lit up the screen. I accepted the call and fell back onto my bed.

"So, how did it go?"

"How did what go?" I asked, scooting back to the headboard and plumping up my pillow.

Dani sighed into the speaker. "Duh. Christmas? Family? Bedroom Girl?"

"Please don't call her Bedroom Girl."

"What? I thought it was a cool nickname, like they do when people are undercover, you know?"

"You watch too much TV."

"You don't watch enough."

I let out a laugh. Dani could argue the sky was green if you gave her half a chance. "Did you have a nice Christmas with Brandon?"

"Oh no, you don't. None of your diversion tactics here."

"What? It was a genuine question."

"I want to know about you first."

I sighed. "Fine. The lowdown is this: Christmas was good, spending time with my family was good, and 'Bedroom Girl'…has a girlfriend."

"*No!* This is so not what Camilla predicted."

Camilla? Why was that name so familiar? "Who's—" The words died in my mouth as my brain worked to fit it together. *Oh, no.* "You spoke to your psychic about me?" I asked incredulously. "Dani, what the hell?"

"I was worried about you! Besides, she was right about the other two things. Your Christmas was good, wasn't it?"

I groaned. "Dani. Please. No more telling Camilla about my poor excuse for a love life."

She hesitated, and my Dani-senses started tingling.

"What is it? What aren't you telling me?"

"Speaking of your poor excuse for a love life… Katie dropped by the office Christmas Eve trying to find you."

My stomach dropped. "No she didn't."

"Oh, yes, she did."

"Alright, enough of the panto dramatics." I rubbed my fingers over my forehead, already feeling an ache coming on at just the mention of my ex-girlfriend. "What did she want?"

"She wanted to see you. Christina was in, sorting some paperwork, and she told her you weren't in, but Katie didn't believe her."

Poor Christina. "What happened?"

"She said she needed to speak with you."

"She really can't take no for an answer."

"I did try to warn you about her. I didn't like the way she spoke about the office fish. I feel like you can tell a lot about a person from the way they treat animals."

"Very true, Dani. But the office fish aren't real. They're robot fish. They don't have feelings."

"You don't know that."

I shook my head, fighting a smile. "Well, then, Mr Clark and the rest of us will be in for a pretty nasty lawsuit at some point."

"And I didn't like how she was trying to change you. She made you wear that awful spotty coat that made you look like Mr Blobby. And she called me plump!"

I winced. Katie had a temper and a severe case of

opening-her-mouth-before-she-thought-itus. As soon as Katie had started badmouthing my friends, that was a major deal breaker for me. We'd only been dating for two months, anyway. I didn't know why she couldn't let it go. I certainly didn't want to get back together.

Dani sighed down the phone. "She seems on a quest to find you—"

I bolted upright. "What! No... Why?"

"I don't know. Have you responded to her recently?"

"No. I've blocked her number now. Hopefully she's got the message."

My headache was back with a vengeance, pulsating in waves. Katie had some boundary issues, that was for sure, and dealing with her shit on top of my own was so not what I needed right now.

Dani perked up. "Anyway, tell me about Bedroom Girl."

"Me and *Vicky* are going to an ice fair today. But before you get any ideas, it's not a date. Just two friends hanging out."

"*Ooh*, an ice fair. How very country of you."

I checked my watch. "Actually, I'd better get going, Dani. I gotta pick her up in thirty minutes."

"Ooh, what're you going to wear? That nice blue Chanel dress I packed for you?"

"I don't think so, it's a bit cold. I'm thinking jeans and a shirt."

She tutted. "You can have anything you want in life if you dress for it."

"Is that another one of your dad's quotes?" I asked.

Dani laughed. "Not this time. The man can box and inspire a crowd, but a fashionista he is not. It's Edith Head."

"Who?"

"She was a famous costume designer."

I shook my head. Dani always had the ability to surprise me. "And how do you know that?"

Her voice rose. "I'll have you know I'm a very educated woman."

She had her moments, that was true, but this was too random. "I'm not buying that."

She sighed. "Fine. I learned it at the pub quiz. But you'd know that if you went with us once in a while."

I laughed. "Okay, I'll go with you next time."

"Maybe with Bedroom Girl?"

My thoughts multiplied, trying to imagine a life where that might be possible. I sighed, squashing those futile hopes down. "No, Dani."

"Okay, I can take a hint. Go have fun. Love you!"

"Love you too."

I hung up and collapsed back on my bed, my head swimming with all the new information. Katie had thrown a bit of a spanner in the works, but I couldn't dwell on that now. I needed a pick-me-up. Perhaps a fancy dress wasn't a bad place to start.

"Hey, Zoodle. What's the weather going to be like today?"

My phone lit up, the little spheres whirring around. *"There's a forty-two percent chance of snow, with a mix of clear and cloudy skies."*

"Are you sure? You did say that yesterday too."

The spheres circled, and then the screen went dark. *Wonderful.*

I dressed in the dress Dani mentioned, a beautiful royal blue cotton that fell just below my knees. My brown hair perfectly teased and curled, mascara and red lipstick on, I turned in the mirror, pleased with my reflection. It felt good to dress up. There was no harm in looking good, right?

I skipped down the stairs, nerves tangling in my belly. Mum stopped dead in the hallway, her mouth agape.

"Bloody hell. Are you off to the King's ball?"

"What? Is it too much?"

"You look beautiful, Holly. But don't forget your coat, you'll bloody freeze to death."

"It's supposed to snow!" Dad called from the living room.

"I've already asked Zoodle. It says there's a forty percent chance."

"Zoodle?" Mum's eyebrows drew together like I'd

just tried to explain Pythagoras' theorem.

"The in-built AI in our phones?" Still met with her look of utter confusion, I sighed, ushering her out of the way so I could put on my black boots. "I don't have time to explain it again."

She huffed, but she moved out of my way, watching me with intrigue as I pulled my zippers up my calves. "You definitely get your style from me."

I glanced up at her, in her dirty, grey jodhpurs and stained orange gilet. "Sure, Mum. Sure."

She crossed her arms. "Well, it's certainly not your father."

"Maybe it was Cameron." I stood and kissed her cheek, catching the surprise flash over her features. "I'll be back in the evening."

I grabbed my keys and stepped out into the December chill, wrapping my black shearling coat tightly around myself, the bird-shit stain long gone, thanks to Mum's cleaning prowess. *I wonder how Harry is doing with Victrolly and the pigeons?*

Before I could even walk up her drive, Vicky opened the door, calling goodbye behind her. I stopped where I was, struck by the sight of her in a fitted mint green shirt and tight black jeans. A thick burgundy coat hung over her arm as she pivoted towards me. It was a simple look but very effective. I suddenly felt overdressed.

She jolted to a halt, slapping her hand across her

chest like she was in a telenovela. "Jesus, Holly. You scared me."

I combed my eyes over her shapely legs, caressed by the denim. "You look…great."

"So do you, Miss Fancy Pants." She flashed me a teasing smile. "My car or yours?"

"Let's go in mine."

"Are you sure? Tanya said it might snow later and"—she glanced at my BMW before raising an eyebrow—"well, I'm going to guess you don't have winter tyres."

"No, but I'm sure we'll be just fine." The mention of Tanya irked me. But I needed to get used to talking about her if we were going to stay friends. I gritted my teeth and swallowed it down. *It'll be just fine, Holly. It'll be just fine.*

Chapter Twenty-Two

The Donnington Ice Fair heaved with people. A huge open-air ice rink took centre stage, surrounded by rows of red plastic seating up to the heavens. It wasn't as spectacular as the posters—or my mother—had suggested, but the atmosphere felt electric. Dusk was beginning to set in, and golden fairy lights flickered to life, guiding our way around the site. We walked linking arms, peering up at the purple clouds as people strolled towards the rink. The smells from the food stalls selling hot chocolates, fresh pretzels, and hot dogs permeated the air. Souvenir shops stocked with T-shirts, hats, water bottles, and stickers were manned by bored teenagers, already waiting for their shifts to be over.

"Bloody hell. Have you seen how much it is for a pretzel?" I leaned into Vicky, watching with jealousy as a grey-haired man passed with one, licking sugar from his fingertips.

"What did you expect? We're not in Mistleberry any more."

I snorted. "Alright, Dorothy."

Vicky pinched my arm, and we sidestepped around a slow-walking couple. "Whatever. Shouldn't you be used to extortionate prices anyway? You live in London."

"True. I just wouldn't expect it here." I pointed at a stall to the left of us. "I mean, look at that. An ice-sculpture lesson. Why would anyone want to do that here? What are we going to do with it afterwards? Carry it to our seats and watch as it melts?"

"It might be a cheaper drink than from the bar."

"That's a good point."

We reached the entrance and fell to the back of the line. I could hardly feel the cold because of the crowds of people, just the heat of Vicky's body pressed to mine. We shuffled forwards, chatter filtering around us.

"So," I started, "where's Tanya tonight?"

Vicky's eyebrows quirked. "She's in London for a shoot."

"How long for?"

"Just the day. She should be back tomorrow."

"Does she normally travel a lot?"

"Yeah, back and forth from London quite a bit. I think that's what's pushing the move."

We edged closer to the front, and I dug around in my bag for our tickets. "That makes sense. Who's the shoot for?"

"New Look." Vicky side-eyed me. "What's with all the questions?"

Before I could answer, we were greeted by a small red-haired man with a full beard. He gave a half-smile, scanned our tickets, and then we were through the doors. People crossed the paths in every direction, chatting and drinking from plastic cups. I spotted the entry to our seats through gaps in the crowd and pulled Vicky along behind me.

"So," she continued, "what's with the third degree?"

"Can I not take an interest in her? She's someone special to you."

Vicky watched me carefully. "And while that's very nice, I don't quite buy it."

I pretended to be offended. "Victoria Ann Castleton, what kind of person do you take me for?"

She drew her brows together, then caught my arm before a tall man could walk into me with his full pint of beer. She steered me through the entryway, and as we walked up the steps to find our seats, she said, "I just feel a bit weird about it. And I know you do too, and we haven't really spoken about it yet."

We found our seats, halfway up and in the middle. Mr Simon must have paid a decent price for them. A loud voice called through the overhead speakers, announcing the show's start in ten minutes. Once settled into the hard plastic—definitely not the soft pleather Mum suspected—Vicky turned to me with a sigh.

"So, what's with all the questions?"

"Fine. Is it so bad to want to know a bit about her, so I can plan her ultimate demise?"

We both burst out laughing, and Vicky shook her head.

I continued, "Joking, of course." *Although maybe not completely.* "Look, I don't want to make anything awkward between us. More than I already have with the kiss…and everything."

"You haven't."

Our eyes met, something sizzling in the air between us. Was she blushing? *Focus, Holly.*

"Well, we can talk about it. About her."

Her gaze drifted over my face. "We don't have to talk about it."

"We do."

"Well, someone's changed their tune."

"You must have caught me on a good day, then."

She smiled and shook her head. "What do you want to know?"

Want was a strong word, but to be a real friend to her, I needed to understand a few things. "What are your plans for the future? Job? The apartment?"

The lights overhead dimmed, and a spotlight shone onto the ice, lighting up a smartly dressed man and woman. *Great. Just perfect timing.*

Vicky leaned across from her seat. "We can continue this conversation later," she whispered, causing the hairs on my arms to tingle.

"Welcome, everyone, to the sixth annual Donnington Ice Fair," the woman announced, shimmying so the sequins on her silver dress sparkled.

Her partner looped his arm around her shoulder. "And do we have a show for you tonight!"

I pushed back into my seat. Watching people skate and dance on the ice would give me some time to think. I wanted to know more about Vicky and Tanya's relationship, but truthfully, it was like drinking acid. Every little detail was hard to swallow.

But I didn't want to run. Just because I struggled to stomach it, didn't mean I should give up.

Loud music fired out from the speakers, bright sparks flew out of cannons, and a parade of skaters glided out onto the ice, each wearing a spectacular colourful outfit. The crowd erupted in applause as the skaters waved while the presenters announced their names.

"Are we supposed to know who these people are?"

Vicky whispered as people screamed and waved their arms frantically.

"I'm not sure. Are they from that show on the telly?"

As though they were listening in, the presenters announced the mix of performers, ranging from Olympic medal winners to ice-dancing show finalists, and even ice and circus acrobats. *Mr Simon did good.* It was an amazing line-up. My worries and thoughts melted away as the show began with a choreographed dance routine. I was mesmerised.

"Do you fancy a go on the ice afterwards?" I asked Vicky after a few rounds of performances. "They open the rink to the public and we can rent skates."

"You sure you're up to it? Won't you injure yourself again?"

"That was the horse's fault, not mine."

She laughed. "Okay, sure." She bumped my shoulder with hers, and heat flushed through my veins.

The skaters completed their routines, wearing beautiful, sparkly outfits as the lights followed them over the ice. Suddenly a rumbling sound drew my head upwards. Thick clouds had rolled over the darkened sky, and the first white snowflakes drifted down, glittering in the spotlights like falling diamonds. The skaters were unbothered by the snow and continued their routines with elegance and poise.

"It looks even more magical like this," Vicky

commented, tipping her head up to the sky.

I couldn't help but agree. It felt like years since I'd seen real snow, and though we hadn't had any in time for Christmas, it was a special moment.

Flakes caught in Vicky's long lashes, and she brushed them out of her hair.

And then the heavens really opened. The slight flurry was multiplied by hundreds of flurries, colouring the sky a foggy white. Visibility dropped, and then one of the skaters caught an edge and fell on the ice with a smack. A collective gasp rolled through the crowd.

The music continued to play through the speakers, but the crowd grew restless as we waited for direction. Snow piled on the ground beneath us, bringing with it a familiar chill.

"What's going on?" I asked, squinting and trying to see through the fog. "I can't see anything."

The people in front of us stood up, the murmurs throughout the rink increasing in volume.

Then an announcement ripped through the speakers. "Attention, everyone. Due to the unforeseen weather circumstances, the rest of this performance is cancelled effective immediately. Please make your way to the exits, and have a safe journey home."

"What? Are they really cancelling? It's only a little bit of snow." I glanced around at the people already leaving their seats. "It'll stop in a bit, it always does."

"It's more than a bit of snow, Hol, and I don't want to get caught out in a blizzard. Come on, let's get out of here."

Disappointment engulfed me. This wasn't how the night was supposed to go. I wanted to learn more about Tanya, get to spend time with Vicky, prove to myself I could do this. I wanted us to enjoy the magic of the ice fair, to skate and maybe even hold hands as we glided around the rink. But the night was over before it had really begun.

Then Vicky grabbed my hand, and sparks ignited at her touch. She pulled me from my seat and started towards the stairs. "I have a feeling it's going to get a little crazy out here. Stay close to me."

I hated the way my body reacted to her; it made it seriously hard to think straight. She weaved through the people all heading for the exits as the snow blanketed us, our hands staying entwined. A surge of people pushed forward, and our grip broke as we left through the doors.

"Vicky!" I scanned the crowd but struggled to see through the falling snowflakes and panicked fans leaving the rink. "Vicky!"

I had to find her. At the rate of the falling snow, I doubt she'd be able to recognise my car, and she'd never be able to walk back to Mistleberry in this weather. It was miles away. I was pushed out through the doors and back into the field outside. The fairy lights cast a golden glow over the snow but didn't help visibility.

Then someone grabbed me.

I spun to find Vicky looking back at me, eyes wide and panicked.

"I told you to stay close to me," she said, her breath coming out in wisps.

"I did, but—"

"Come on, let's get to your car before it gets any worse." She interlinked her fingers in mine, and we hurried back past the stalls all the way to the car park. When people pushed and shoved us, I pulled Vicky close to me, squishing our bodies together, and breathed her in. The night wasn't going too badly after all.

The car park was chaos. Cars were spinning in all directions, kicking up snow everywhere. The ground was completely covered. Worse, the cold was seeping into my coat, making me shiver.

"Fuck." Vicky sighed, turning to me. "Your car isn't going to get out of here, is it?"

"I d—d—doubt it."

Her eyebrows pinched together. "Your coat isn't waterproof, either?"

I shook my head.

Vicky tutted. "Honestly, Holly, you leave the countryside for two minutes and forget what the weather can get like here." She glanced around her, taking in all the commotion. Her eyes lit up. "Let's go. I know a place."

"But my car—"

She squeezed my hand before tucking both hers and mine into her warm coat pocket. "It's not far, we don't need your car. But we've got to move fast."

"No 'I told you so'?"

"Oh, the 'I told you so' is definitely implied. We'll discuss that later." She grinned and led me into the swirling blizzard, anchored by the weight of her warm hand in mine.

Chapter Twenty-Three

The snow continued to fall all around us, the wind blowing it sideways like tiny missiles into our faces. I tried to shield myself from the cold, but my favourite coat wasn't doing the most stellar job.

Vicky led the way down the street as cars attempting to leave the site spun their wheels, sliding all over the roads. There was no way people were going to be getting out of here that way; the tarmac was completely covered. It was typical of England not to be prepared for the snowfall, especially in the countryside. Some things never changed.

"Where are we going?" I asked, shielding my face

inside my coat. "Please don't tell me we're walking all the way back to Mistleberry?"

"In these shoes? Not a chance."

I noticed other people heading the same way as us. "So where?"

"There's a new hotel down here. We should be able to get a room for the night."

"That's your big plan?" I hated to admit that the idea of sharing a room with Vicky flooded my belly with excitement. "How do you know so much about Donnington?"

As soon as the question left my lips, I realised the answer, but Vicky took a few seconds to reply. "Tanya's family owns the hotel. I'm sure we can sort something out."

The excitement in my stomach soured. But at the rate the snow was falling, I didn't see another option. "You sure there's not anywhere else?" I joked.

"Not anywhere where we might be able to pull a favour. Unless you want to walk around in this all night?" She tugged me left down a side street, where the Bellchester Hotel stood proud in all its glory, a white stone building declaring its presence with a bright sign above its shiny, red door. We pushed it open, finding immediate relief from the hot air blowing out above the entrance.

"Goodness. Are you two ladies alright?" a blonde

receptionist asked, pulling her dark eyebrows together.

Vicky put her bag on the desk, casting snow everywhere. "Oh god, I'm sorry."

"It's alright." The receptionist picked up a cloth from inside a drawer and swiped it across the top. The crow's feet around her eyes deepened, suggesting she wanted to dust off the two of us as well. "Have you got a reservation?"

"We haven't, but—"

"I'm sorry. We're fully booked tonight with the Donnington Ice Fair." She pursed her lips, the pink lipstick cracking. I glanced at her nametag: Jane.

"I understand. That's where we've just come from, but they've cancelled the show early because of the weather."

Jane frowned. "I'm sorry to hear that. Unfortunately, there's nothing I can do."

As the snow on my coat melted, it seeped further into my skin, making me shiver. I moved back towards the door and stood under the heating. I could just make out their conversation under the soft buzz of the air system.

"I'm sure my girlfriend could sort something out," Vicky said, leaning forward.

The receptionist looked over Vicky's shoulder at me and raised an eyebrow. "I sincerely doubt it."

Excuse me?

I looked down at my sodden shoes, legs and coat. My

hair was probably in a state of disarray, and though this coat was one of the most expensive things I owned, even that looked like I'd found it in a skip at this point. *Okay, fair enough.*

"Tanya Jones?" Vicky continued. "If I call my girlfriend and tell her I'm waiting at the Bellchester with Jane, do you think she could find me a room?"

"Miss Jones?" Jane glanced at me again, but with confusion this time. "But this isn't Miss Jones."

Excuse me, "this"? Who is she calling "this"?

If I'd had the energy, I would have stormed over and given her a piece of my mind. But the hot air was amazing, and I couldn't do anything other than stand under its magical glow.

"That's my friend. I'm talking about my girlfriend, Tanya Jones. Shall I call her?"

Jane's eyes widened so much a vein snaked across her forehead, threatening to burst. "Er, no, no. Let me just have a check for you. We usually have something saved in case one of the Joneses is in town." She typed on her keyboard, her eyes flashing across the screen. "I will have to confirm some details first, though, with the family."

"No problem." Vicky turned back to me and smiled, giving me a thumbs up.

I returned the gesture, but my mind struggled to comprehend what I'd just witnessed. The Joneses had trees reserved, rooms too. What else was strictly their space in my own town? Tanya was even buying an apartment in London, my second home. I was suddenly hyper-aware of Tanya. Everything I saw around me belonged to her. Even the air at this point. I felt very out of place.

After the check was complete, the keys had been handed over, and Jane had apologised fifty-six times for our inconvenience, we made our way down the corridor to the lift, feet squelching as we went.

"That must be a useful trick to pull," I commented, as Vicky pressed the button. "Name-dropping your girlfriend."

The lift doors opened, and we stepped inside. She pressed the third floor, the highest in the boutique hotel.

"It was interesting to see you behave like that," I continued, the mirror in the lift reflecting my discomfort. "Like you're entitled to something because of your connections."

"I think that's a bit uncalled for." Vicky pressed her lips together before continuing with a huff. "What would you suggest we do? Stay out in your BMW and freeze to death? If we'd taken my car, we'd probably be fine, but now we're snowed in."

"I could've called my dad."

She turned to me. "You'd want to risk him driving in the blizzard?" The doors chimed and opened, and we stepped out into the hallway. It still smelled of fresh paint.

"No, but—"

"You're so stubborn, Holly. And you act like you're so different from Tanya, but you're more similar than you think."

That angered me. "The only thing alike about us is we're both from the city, a place you claim to hate so much. You've teased me about it all week, but it can't be that bad if you're considering moving there."

She stopped outside a door that read 307 and flashed the card in front of the reader. It clicked, flashed green, and she pushed the door open.

"I'm not talking about that; I don't know what I'm doing yet. I mean the clothes you wear. The jealousy. That damn stubbornness."

I followed her into a beautiful red and gold hotel room. A large double bed, with crisp white bedsheets, took up the centre. Two wooden dressers and two wardrobes lined the walls, and a huge green plant nestled in the corner. All I saw was Tanya. Anger bubbled in my gut. I tore my focus away from the painting hanging over the bed and faced Vicky, but her back was to me. "Jealousy?"

"Yes. Jealousy."

"Well, that's one way to throw my feelings for you back in my face."

Vicky's shoulders sunk, but she didn't turn around.

The anger spread into my chest. "And you're one to

talk about jealousy, Vicky. What about Billy? What about prom night?"

She faced me, her eyes narrowing. "That's different and you know it."

I threw my hands up in the air. "Why is it? It's the same situation from where I'm standing. If anything, this is worse."

"Worse?" she said, on the exhale. "What, because we were younger then? You don't think it hurts as much? I cried myself to sleep for weeks after prom. I didn't know if I'd ever be able to look at you in the same way ever again."

My heart plummeted. "Vicky—"

"You broke my heart when you chose him." There was an uncomfortable silence between us. The sadness in Vicky's eyes twisted my stomach.

"I broke my own heart too." Tears pricked my eyelids, and I swallowed. "I was scared. Terrified of my feelings for you. I still am. The way I feel about you makes me feel certifiably insane sometimes." I shivered, chills creeping up my spine. Part of me didn't care, didn't even feel the cold; the ache in my chest consumed most of my brain power. "I used to be scared of who I was, but I'm not any more. I'm not scared of those feelings for you. Even when I don't want to feel them, they're there, Vicky. I can't ever turn those off. I'm trying to be your friend. I'm trying. I am—"

The tears fell, sliding down my cheeks, and I turned away from her.

"I know you're trying, Hol. I can see that."

I glanced back. Vicky's eyes were glossed over.

It was a few moments before she spoke again, her voice barely audible. "But how can I trust you? That you won't break my heart?"

My heart raced, thumping so hard inside my chest I thought I might be sick. "I don't know," I said quietly. If she didn't trust me, couldn't see I was laying my heart out for her on a silver platter, I didn't know what to say. "Maybe that's all we'll do. Break each other's hearts. I'm not sure we can even help it." I brushed my tear-stained cheeks on the sleeve of my coat, but it was soaking wet and freezing cold.

"You should shower," she said lifelessly. "There are robes in the wardrobe. I'll get someone to dry our clothes."

"Okay."

I opened the door to the bathroom and peeled my coat down my sodden arms. Another violent shiver ripped up my spine. I was afraid to let the cold in, afraid of what it might do to all my progress.

My mind blurred. How had we got to this moment? Just a few hours ago, we were laughing and having a good time. Now I couldn't see any way out of this mess—and we were stuck in the same room together for the night.

Just great.

I shut the bathroom door and let the hot shower scald my skin, trying to feel anything other than the black hole expanding inside my heart.

Chapter Twenty-Four

Vicky and I hadn't spoken since I came out of the shower. I lay on one side of the bed in my white towel bathrobe, listening to the sounds of Vicky in the bathroom. I considered what I'd do if we were both single. It only took me two seconds to know I'd walk in there and tell her I didn't want to keep fighting. I'd tell her that my feelings for her were real, that there was nothing else I was more sure about. I'd press her up against the wall and kiss her, let the water wash any further trepidation away.

But it was torture to replay such daydreams. If Vicky only wanted to be friends, I had to let it go. I had to squash those feelings down. I just didn't know if I could do it any more.

The water stopped.

My heart thudded in my chest as footsteps pattered across the floor. The door opened, and Vicky stepped out, blonde hair wet and swept back, an identical white robe to mine wrapped around her perfect body. I couldn't look away, but I probably should have, judging by the look on her face.

"Didn't anyone tell you it's rude to stare?" she said dryly, waiting beside the bed with one hand on her hip.

My emotions swirled as I took her in. "You're so very beautiful, you know."

Vicky's demeanour softened, her arms dropping to her sides. She climbed onto the bed next to me, keeping a sizeable distance between us. "You are too, Holly. I've always thought that."

I sighed, pulling my gaze away from her legs and trying to focus on a place that was safer. I settled on her neck, but a memory jumped into my mind: us kissing under her duvet when we were teenagers. Our hands exploring and tongues tracing over skin. Heat flared in my core, and I looked away. Her neck was definitely not a safe place.

"What is it?" she asked.

"Just remembering something."

"What?"

"Nothing."

"Oh, come on. You can't do that."

I looked back at her. Her blue eyes were enchanting under the warm light. She was so much the Vicky I knew before. Same bone structure and freckles, a cute little nose that scrunched whenever she really laughed. The same eyes that made me question everything about myself. The same mouth that had kissed me and shown me everything I'd been missing.

But she was different too. More sure of herself. Confident. Qualities that suited her, but in ways that made me feel obsolete. If Vicky didn't need me, what was my purpose? If she didn't trust me, could we even be friends?

"Remember your dad's birthday?" I asked. "When we went to the cinema to watch that weird karate film?"

"Yeah. What about it?" I waited for the realisation to roll across her face. "Oh." Her attention dropped to my mouth before bouncing back up to meet my eyes.

I sighed, feeling myself sucked into the nostalgia. "I think I knew then that I'd always feel this way about you. I think that's what really terrified me the most. How I had no control over it." I thumbed over the robe's belt, avoiding her gaze. It felt good to finally talk about it, but I still couldn't meet the look in her eyes. I knew I'd stop; the fear would get me. "Do you ever think of it?"

Once the question was out there, my stomach rolled. I wanted to take it back. Whichever way she answered was only going to torture me.

"Think of that night?" Vicky said. "Or about us?"

I sucked in a shaky breath and let it go. "Both. Either."

"Yes. Of course I do. I still live next door to your parents. It would be pretty impossible not to think about you."

"You know that's not what I meant." I forced myself to meet her gaze.

Her eyes studied my face, but her jaw was locked, her expression unreadable.

She swallowed, her blue pools watering. Now it was her turn to look away. "I held onto everything for a long time, Hol. But it hurt to see you living your life without me. I was always waiting, holding onto a small sliver of hope. Counting down the days until you'd come and visit. After Cameron…I thought you'd move home for good. But you never called me back or answered my messages. It was like you didn't care."

I shook my head. "That's not fair. I did. I do. I care about you so much. I was just so wrapped up in myself and selfish—"

"Hey, it's okay, I understand. I don't blame you for it. We all react differently. I tried to give you space to grieve…but I was grieving too." She paused and sniffed. "I needed you too." She tried to blink away tears, but they trickled down her cheeks.

Without thinking, I pulled her to me, wrapping my

arms around her tight. My heart ached. I had no idea how badly I'd hurt her. But there was nothing I could've done. I was barely alive myself after finding out about Cameron's death.

"I'm sorry," I whispered into her hair, holding her tighter.

"I know you are."

"And I'm here now."

She cried into my robe, and I rocked her quietly, the snow still falling outside the window. Tears slid down my cheeks, and I brushed them away with my shoulder.

"I had to stop myself from thinking of you," she said quietly. So softly, I barely heard it. "I couldn't wait forever."

"It's okay, Vicky. It's okay." I pressed a kiss to her head and breathed her in. I was lost in so many different feelings, I couldn't focus on one enough to form any other words. But it felt good to hold her, to finally clear the air between us. It was a long time overdue.

We stayed like that for a while. The reverse of the time Vicky had held me in her arms. I wondered if she'd felt as protective of me as I did of her. I wanted us to stay that way forever so I could shield her from all the bad in the world. But I still couldn't protect her from me and all the hurt I'd caused her. That stung.

Even though I'd never intended to, knowing I'd caused her pain cut me open. I didn't want to be the reason for her sadness. The soft, weeping woman in my arms didn't deserve any more upset. If she was happy with Tanya, who was I to judge? I'd not exactly been a shining example of what to do in life. I wanted to do the right thing. I just didn't know what that was.

Three sharp knocks on the door made us both jump.

"That must be our clothes," Vicky mumbled.

"That's a shame. I'll miss the robe look on you."

Vicky gave me a look. "Even now, you can't resist a flirty comment, can you?"

I forced a small smile. "Guilty."

Vicky rose to open the door, thanked the man for our clothes, and closed it behind her. She raised them in a defeated gesture, her eyes betraying the emotions on her face. Was she feeling the ache in her chest like I was?

If this was all we did to each other, it was best to move on. What moving on entailed exactly, I didn't know. How was I supposed to get over my first love? My heart tried to argue with me, but I shut it out. I wasn't listening any more. I was tired.

We got changed back into our fresh clothes and slipped into bed. The atmosphere had changed between us, like the heavy air had settled in our bones, sapping all our energy. A soft light came from Vicky's bedside table, but the rest of the room was in darkness. The snow was supposed to stop in a few hours, and then once the roads were cleared I should be able to get my car out. Part of me wished for the snow to keep falling so we wouldn't have to leave this room and face the fact that it was over between us. But I knew we'd have to leave eventually. *Nothing lasts forever.*

I adjusted myself in the bed, rolling onto my side so I could look at her profile. Memories of many a sleepover flicked into my mind, each blurring into the other as though playing on a carousel. I felt simultaneously comfortable and awkward in her presence now; something I'd never felt in all the years I'd known her. But I still wanted to reach out and trace her lips with mine. That hadn't changed. The urge to pull her close to me and not let go.

However, just like when I was younger, I was too afraid, but this time for a whole different reason.

Vicky was looking up at the ceiling, unaware of my staring, lost in the tangle of her own thoughts. I wished I knew exactly how she was feeling. All this talking was new to me.

"Hey," I said softly, my voice too loud for the quiet room. "You never answered me before. About your plans for the future."

Vicky blew out a breath. "Really? You want to know about that now?"

"Just be honest with me. I'm a big girl, Vicky, I can handle it."

"Maybe you can, but I'm not sure I can. My head is

a mess."

There were a few beats of silence between us. I watched the steady rise and fall of her chest. "Well, do you still want to go into business? I could still put in a good word for you at Pertoni Clark."

She pressed her lips together. "Tanya's dad offered me a job."

Her words lingered in the air. A job...an apartment...a whole life with Tanya. "Oh." I swallowed. "And do you want to take it?"

"I don't know. It's hard to know what the right thing to do is."

"If I'm honest, you don't seem to be a fan of the city life."

She snorted. "I guess you could say that. But if it worked for you, maybe it'll work for me. Who knows?"

"Do you think you're both moving too fast?"

She turned her head towards me. "I'm not sure you're the best person for me to discuss this with."

"I used to be."

"Well, things change, don't they? We're not the same kids we once were, Holly. There's no denying that."

More silence. I bit my lip, debating whether I should speak my mind. *This might be my last chance to do so.*

"I had a relationship like that."

Vicky rolled over so we were facing each other. "What do you mean 'like that'?"

Oh, god. Not a good start. "My ex, Katie, it moved way too fast. I don't think she really wanted me but wanted to shape me into someone that she wanted."

"And you think that's what Tanya is doing?" There was an edge to her voice.

"I don't know her well enough," I answered honestly. "But I think you do know her. And that you know in your heart if it's right or not."

"You're right. You don't know her well enough." Her eyebrows furrowed, creasing her forehead. "Yes, we don't have that much in common, and she's always busy, but she's a nice person, Holly."

"I'm just looking out for you."

"Are you?"

I studied her face. Her soft eyes were still full of kindness, even when she was angry. I admired the sprinkle of freckles across her cheeks and her small, round nose. "Yes. I am. You're an amazing person, Vicky. I don't think you should have to change for anyone. Don't sacrifice what you want to please someone else. You deserve to be happy."

Her gaze flicked over my face for a few moments. "I'm not accepting less. But sometimes we have to make sacrifices. Compromise. Nothing is ever perfect."

"That's true. But don't compromise who you are. What your dreams are. What kind of life you want."

She pressed her lips together into a tight line. It was

a while before she spoke again. "Well, what about you? What are your dreams now? What kind of life do you want?"

"Bloody hell." I let out a laugh, and Vicky mirrored it.

"You can't honestly think you're going to get away without spilling any of your secrets, Hol."

"I think most of mine are out there already." The smiles slipped from our faces. The air was charged now with a different kind of tension. I was the first to look away. I couldn't handle the rollercoaster of emotions between us tonight. I sighed. "Honestly, I've been thinking about moving closer to home."

"Really?" Vicky couldn't hide the surprise on her face. "Why?"

"Well, when I think about what kind of life I want, I want to be able to say I made my family proud. That I lived my life *mostly* without regret. I obviously can't change the past. But I can make up for it in the future."

"But is that what you want, or what your parents want?"

I rolled the question through my mind. "It's what I want. Time with my family. London hasn't felt like home for a long while now."

Vicky seemed to mull this over. "So I might be moving just as you come back? Isn't that just exceptional timing?"

I smiled. "Isn't it just."

She groaned, covering her face with her hands. "Wow. This is a lot for one night. Donnington Fair sure knows how to show people a good time."

I laughed. "It's not been so bad."

"What a ringing endorsement."

I knocked her playfully. "You know what I mean."

She nodded, a modest smile playing on her lips. "Anyway, we should probably get some sleep. It could be a long walk home in the morning, or a lot of digging in the snow."

"Yeah, you're right." Something sunk in my chest. I didn't want the night to end. As awful as it had been in parts, it felt like a weight had been lifted. With my heart out on the table, I didn't want to have to cram it back into its cage again.

Vicky rolled over to turn out the light, and then everything was draped in blackness.

"Goodnight, Holly."

"Sweet dreams, Vicky."

I shuffled in bed, trying to get comfy, but my feet were too cold. My head was swimming; the sound of my own breathing irritated me. My pulse thumped away, making me restless.

"Are you okay?" she whispered, her voice soft and angelic.

I closed my eyes for a moment. All I wanted to do

was hold her, to pull her close and soak up her warmth. I thought about our moment earlier and how quickly it'd slipped away. I craved her touch, not even in a sexual way, just to feel anchored and safe. But we couldn't cross that line here. Cuddling in bed was definitely off-limits. "I'm…just a little cold," I managed.

"Oh. Do you wanna warm your feet on mine?"

I smiled into my pillow. "Just like old times. You…sure you don't mind?"

"Just for a little while."

I shuffled myself closer, placing my feet on hers.

She recoiled. "Bloody hell. You're like ice!"

"You're like an oven."

"You're welcome."

"Thank you." The heat from her touch immediately made me feel better. I let out a sigh, forcing my breathing to fall into a steady rhythm.

"I'll bill you tomorrow," she commented. "A fiver an hour."

I chuckled. "Deal."

"Time to sleep now."

I smiled to myself, wanting to keep this moment alive forever. But I knew that it, too, would have to end sometime. I snuggled in a little closer, letting myself indulge in the feeling of her. If this were the last time we'd share a bed, I wanted to remember every last detail. I let out a breath of contentment.

"Goodnight, Vicky."

Chapter Twenty-Five

The drive home was quiet. The staff at Donnington Fair had cleared most of the car park by the time we got there, which was a relief, and the gritters had passed by in the early morning to salt the roads. Grey fluffy clouds were clustered in the sky above, but the snow held off for now.

I'd woken with my arm wrapped around Vicky; our bodies had somehow gravitated into the centre of the bed, despite all the extra room. I wanted to say that it meant something. That our bodies had pulled together like magnets, in the absence of our minds there to overcomplicate things. But maybe it was just the human physiological need for warmth. Maybe it was nothing special at all.

Vicky hummed along to "The Little Drummer Boy" on the radio, looking out of the window as we drove through the country roads back to Mistleberry. Surprisingly, the roads nearer home had been cleared, with large lumps of snow piled up on either side of the tarmac. I still took a steady pace, though. I had a bad feeling curdling in my gut. It felt like we'd finally made progress, but now time was slipping away. In two days, I was going back to London.

New Year's Eve felt like a ticking time bomb. Not a celebration.

The familiar sound of "All I Want For Christmas is You" trickled through the speakers, and Vicky groaned, tipping her head back into the headrest.

"What's wrong?"

"I *hate* this song," she said through gritted teeth.

"What? You can't be serious. It's the best Christmas song in the whole world." I shot her a glance to see if she was joking, but the grimace on her face told a different story.

"You try listening to this on repeat for eight hours, and then we can talk about it."

"Why would you do that to yourself?"

"Not through choice." Manic eyes glared at me. "I worked in a supermarket in my second year at uni, and they used to torture us with the Christmas CD on repeat." She looked back out the window. "If I ever see Mariah Carey…she'd better run."

I burst out laughing, but Vicky snapped her head towards me. "I'm not joking. I was cross-country champion for three years. She'd better be quick."

"And that was like fifteen years ago."

"Hey. I've still got it."

I bet you do.

I cranked the volume up a couple of notches and laughed like a villain as Vicky shook her head.

"Please, no, Holly! I'll jump out of this car."

I sang along badly with the chorus, my vocal range nowhere near as good as Mariah's. Vicky put her hands over her ears, to block out my singing or the song, I wasn't certain. I turned onto our street as the last chords faded, drawing out the last note in an agonising alto.

"Honestly, I'm just sad I didn't discover your hate for this song sooner. How have we not heard it yet?"

"It had been a Christmas miracle." Vicky sighed as I switched off the engine, the car immediately filling with quiet as the heaters shut off. "But in a few more days, the Christmas songs will go back into hiding, and everything will be safe again."

I snorted. "You're so dramatic."

"You don't know what I've been through."

I caught her eye, and we both burst out laughing.

"Okay, yeah," she conceded. "Just a tad dramatic."

I grinned at her, flutters multiplying in my belly when she returned the gesture. "I'll make sure to play it at least once a day until I leave."

"You're the devil."

A slamming door drew our attention. Fear jumped up my spine when I saw who was charging towards me. It couldn't be. It couldn't. Was it?

"Where the hell have you been?" The sound was dampened by the glass, but the venom in her voice was unmistakable.

"Oh, god," I muttered. "This is going to be bad."

Katie stomped towards me, waving her arms around like a wild goose about to attack. Her blonde hair was pinned up, showing off those lovely cheekbones I used to admire. Her pink-lipsticked mouth was frozen in a snarl.

This is going to be really bad.

I got out of the car, trying to stay calm. The last thing I needed was for Katie to lose her temper. She'd a temper like a trapped wasp in a glass. "Katie, what are you doing here?"

"What am I doing here? What are you doing here? This is the last place I thought I'd find you."

That hurt a little, but I tried not to let it show. Had I really been that averse to returning home?

"You've been ignoring my texts and calls, what else was I supposed to do?"

"Not…turn up at my parents' house!" I squeezed my fists, trying to push down the anger building up inside. This was such terrible timing.

The slam of a car door told me Vicky had followed. The narrowing of Katie's eyes was also a good indicator.

"And who's this?" she snapped. "Your new bit on the side? Didn't take you long."

Oh my, sweet Mary and Joseph. I wanted the ground to open and swallow me up. Or the blizzard to come back and just blow me away. "That's none of your business. And she's not my 'bit on the side', she's…a friend."

Katie crossed her arms and harrumphed. "Like I'd believe that."

I daren't look at Vicky. The embarrassment might just be enough to kill me.

"Katie," I said, exasperated. "What do you want?" Before she could answer, I held up my hands. "Actually, let's go inside. I think we've given the neighbours enough of a show." When she didn't move, I sighed. "Please."

"Fine." She stomped back to the door but didn't open it. Instead, she turned to us and waited. She obviously wasn't going to give us any privacy.

"And who is this delightful woman?" Vicky asked, her gaze flicking between the two of us.

"My ex," I said. There were so many other things I could say, but they crumpled up and died in my throat. I met Vicky's eyes, full of so many emotions it was hard to

221

stomach. "I'll see you later." I headed towards the house, catching a huff from Vicky on the way.

I don't think that went down well.

Inside the house, I wanted to scream. Butterbee sprinted down the hallway towards me, and I dropped down to greet her. She let out little squeals of delight, making me smile. Dogs always made things better.

Then I caught Katie's scowl. And then my mother's behind her.

I am definitely getting an earful later.

"Did you not get any of my messages?" she asked, keeping her distance in the kitchen.

"No. Sorry. My phone died."

"Everything alright?" She gave me a pointed look. I dreaded to think what kind of conversations had gone on between the two of them. What was I supposed to say? *Everything is splendid, Mum. Can't you see my ex-girlfriend shouting at me in front of the woman I love?*

Love.

Holy shit. Where did that come from?

"It's a bit complicated, Mum, but we'll sort it. Don't worry." I turned to Katie. "I assume you two have already met?"

Mum chuntered something under her breath, but I couldn't hear it. Her scowl told me everything I needed to know.

"Let's go upstairs." I gestured for Katie to lead the

way. She eyed me with contempt but did as asked, taking in the various photo frames hanging on the wall.

"Is this your brother?" she asked, peering at a school picture of the two of us.

I smiled at my toothless grin, Cameron's arm looped over my shoulder. "Yeah."

"He's cute." She continued up the stairs, and we went into my bedroom. I chose to ignore her comment.

I winced at the mess I'd left in the rush to get ready for the Ice Fair yesterday.

Katie raised her eyebrows, moving a pile of discarded clothes on my bed so she could sit down. Whatever. It wasn't as if I was trying to impress her anyway. That ship had long sailed.

"You have a cute home here," she said, her gaze moving around my bedroom, taking it all in. "It's not my taste, obviously, but it's homey."

"Thanks." I leaned against my dresser, wanting to keep my distance. "Katie, why are you here?"

She clenched her fists, her voice raising several notes. "Do you know how frustrating you are? Why haven't you been returning my calls? Is it so fucking difficult to answer your phone?" She closed her eyes and forced out a breath. "Sweet potato fries," she whispered.

What?

Her eyes opened again, and she pinned me with her stare.

Whatever she is planning to do with a potato can only be bad news for me.

Instead of being attacked with a vegetable, I saw how Katie's face had softened, her bottom lip jutting out slightly. The switch in her behaviour had me on edge. She had a perfect palette of manipulation tactics. The cute bottom lip pout was one of them that featured often in our arguments. But the potato was a new one. "Do you know how hurtful it is to be ignored by you? Texts, calls, everything…like nothing ever happened?" She looked up at me, snaring me in those brown doe-eyes. "Do you really hate me that much?"

I sighed, knotting my fingers in front of me so I didn't fidget. "I don't hate you. Our relationship was…complicated, yes, but I don't hate you. I just think it's best, for both of us, to leave that in the past. I don't think we should get back together."

Confusion flashed across her face. "What do you mean?"

Holy Moses. Do I really have to explain this again? I exhaled, searching for the right words. Firm but gentle. I didn't want anything set on fire on her way out. Or potatoes put places they didn't belong. "We're not right for each other, Katie. You want to go out partying and drinking with your friends, and I'm past that stage of my life now. There's nothing wrong with that. We're just…different. We want different things."

"Yeah, I know," she snapped, drawing her eyebrows together. "Why would you think I want to get back together?"

My mouth dropped open. I tried to mask it and brushed my hands through my hair in disbelief. "Because you've been calling and texting me non-stop, showing up at my office, turning up at my *parents'* house, for god's sake. If you don't want to get back together then…why are you here?"

She shook her head, flinging herself back on the bed. She muttered some more nonsense about garlic dip and then righted herself, some loose strands falling out of her bun. "I came to say sorry."

To what, now? "What? But you—"

"Please, let me finish."

I pressed my lips together. This woman was unbelievable. If she'd wanted to say sorry, she could've just said it in a text before it got this far.

"I wanted to say sorry because everything you said about me when we broke up was right. I was selfish and controlling and trying to change you, and that wasn't cool. I can see that now. And I'm working on it." She smiled and laid her hands on her knees. "Just like I'm working through my anger management—I'm actually seeing a counsellor now."

Oh. I wasn't expecting that. However, I could say that her coming all this way wasn't exactly a ringing endorsement of her progress. But I supposed she was trying. I blew out a breath. "Good for you. I'm happy you're doing better."

She held up a finger. "I'm not done."

I resisted the urge to roll my eyes. She always had a knack for sassiness.

"You have my grandma's necklace," she continued. "I'd like that back, please."

"What necklace?"

"I left it on your nightstand. The silver one. With the little locket?"

The realisation dawned on me. "Right, yeah. I also have some of your other stuff too. It's in the car."

She clapped her hands together. "Great."

"You came all the way here for the necklace? I could've just sent it to you."

She nodded. "I know. But my therapist and I agreed it's a good idea to face some of my issues head-on. No running away."

I'd argue that hounding people probably wasn't the greatest advice, either. "Well…that's good, I suppose."

Her voice rose, almost splitting my eardrums. "Plus, it's Christmas! I may have got carried away with the idea of doing something big and starting fresh…but that's what binging Hallmark movies does to you." She shrugged. "Oh, well."

I didn't really know what to say to that. "And

the…potato stuff?"

Her eyes lit up. "Whenever I get angry, it's good for me to focus on my stomach. My anger is closely linked with food, it seems. It helps me stay calm."

I couldn't tell if she was pulling my leg or not. I just smiled and hoped for the best.

"I think you'd benefit too, you know."

Her directness caught me off guard. "What do you mean?"

"From speaking to someone. A therapist. A professional." She offered a small smile. "I know you hate to talk about your brother. But I think it would help."

I chewed my lip. "I've realised recently just how bad I let myself get. You might have a point." I shook my head. "Look at you, giving stellar life advice. Who'd have thought."

"And you thought I wanted to get back together."

"Well, all the phone calls didn't exactly scream 'calm and collected'."

"Yeah, I can see that." Katie let her gaze wander around my room again, as if she could see beneath it. I stilled at the sudden vulnerability on her face. She blew out a long, extended breath. "You know, I think it would do more harm than good…to have you around while I work on myself. You always did manage to get under my skin way too easily." She gave a small smile. "So despite my two hundred phone calls"—my slight wince made her grimace—"after I leave, I'll be deleting your number."

I stared at her in surprise. "I understand." And I did. It was really hard to be around someone you had feelings for while trying to put yourself back together, but it felt good to get closure.

We shared a look of mutual understanding, then Katie stood up suddenly. "So, if I could have my stuff back, I'll be on my way. I'm going to a concert tonight, and I need to get back home."

"Oh, yeah, sure."

Outside, with her bag of stuff in her hand, Katie glanced around at all the snow. "It really is nice here. It suits you, country life."

"I feel like you're mocking me."

A grin crept onto her face. "And you would be right. There's literally nothing here. What do you do all day?"

I laughed. "I don't really know, to be honest."

She nodded. "So...any chance you could give me a lift to the station?"

Chapter Twenty-Six

After Katie had left, Mum was still in a huff with me. Surprisingly, my ex showing up unannounced and staying over in my old bedroom had not put her in the best mood. Apparently, Katie had used her "best soap" and not changed the empty roll of toilet paper. I hadn't really known how to respond to that.

My aunties and uncles had come around for the annual Christmas catch-up, and in between Mum's stomping and unimpressed glares and Dad and Uncle Kevin competing for the Worst Jokester of the Year, I needed some quiet time.

With my bedding in the wash—sleeping in a bed that

smelled like my ex didn't appeal to me much—and the rest of the house already occupied, I snuck out the back door and wandered across to Mr Simon's house, careful not to slip on the snow.

The Christmas tree was still blinking away in the window. Before I could knock, he opened the door, a smile stretching across his face.

"This is a nice surprise." His smile faltered a little, his bushy eyebrows pinching together. "Is everything alright?"

"Yeah, fine. I just wondered if I could come in? My family are all here, and if I hear one more joke about a mince pie, I'll scream."

"Of course." He stepped aside for me to enter. "Alan certainly has a fondness for those cracker jokes."

"Unfortunately he's not the only one."

I wiped my shoes on the welcome mat and removed them, placing them neatly next to Mr Simon's. His smile signalled his approval, and then we ducked into the living room.

"Eggnog?" he offered.

"No, thank you. I think I'm ready for the festive season to be over."

He hesitated, conflicting emotions rolling across his face. "Yeah, I er, heard the commotion earlier."

I sighed. I bet the whole street heard it. That would provide the neighbours with enough gossip for a while, at least. "Just a bit of a misunderstanding."

"Righto. None of my beeswax, anyhoo." He hovered, twisting his hands together. "Could I get you something else? Juice? Water, maybe?"

"Water's fine, thanks."

"Great." He clapped his hands and disappeared into the kitchen.

I spotted Mabel on the sofa, sprawled out lazily with her white belly angled to the ceiling. I brushed my fingers through her soft fur and smiled as she purred lightly. My gaze caught on a familiar face—or three—resting on the mantelpiece, next to the entourage of Mabel photos. The picture of Cameron and me looked back. A warm feeling spread inside my chest. Mr Simon had placed us right there on his mantelpiece. It was so darn cute, I was almost welling up. Then my eyes snared on an unfamiliar photo, one that wasn't there a few days ago. The kind brown eyes sparked distant memories in my mind. Judy, Mr Simon's late wife.

A lump formed in my throat.

"I thought about what you said," Jeff said from behind me. "About keeping Cameron's memory alive." I turned to him, but his attention was on the photo. "I'd hate Judy to think I was hiding her away. I don't want her to ever think that. I could never."

"Hey." I laid a hand on his shoulder, but he still didn't look at me. "We all deal with grief in our own ways.

It's okay."

"I know. But I like having her picture up. It's like she's watching over us. Ain't that right, Mabel?" He bobbed his head, then he remembered the glass in his hand and handed it to me. "Would you like to watch some TV?"

I smiled. "That sounds great."

Afterwards, feeling rejuvenated enough to face the onslaught of questions from my family about my relationships and plans for parenthood, I stepped out into the street.

A soft flurry of snow fell from the skies, but the road was quiet, save for the hum of a few cars in the distance. A calm peace descended on me, quite the opposite of the chaos of the night before. Vicky stayed at the forefront of my mind. I wondered how she was feeling about everything. With New Year's Eve looming, I needed to make my decision whether to go to the party or not. It'd be my last chance to spend time with her.

All my cards were on the table, and I could accept that. It was better to have her in my life as a friend than nothing at all. Not ideal, but sometimes life was shitty, and that's a fact. There's no sugarcoating it or covering it in chocolate and sprinkles. Sometimes people die or they don't love you back, and that's just the way it is.

As I approached the drive, Vicky's front door opened, and my heart leaped. It died in my throat just as fast as Tanya's long legs striding towards me.

"Hey, Holly, I was hoping to run into you." She glanced around at the falling snow. "It's beautiful, isn't it?"

I nodded. "Beats being caught in a blizzard, that's for sure."

"Yes, thank god you were able to sort something out. That was lucky."

If she was fishing for a thank you, she'd be waiting a long time. It might be childish, but I didn't care.

"Anyway, Vicky said you weren't sure if you were going to come to the New Year's Eve party or not." She looked at me expectantly, but I wasn't sure where she was going with this.

"Yeah, I'm not sure yet."

Tanya sighed. "I know we haven't had much chance to spend time with one another, and I'm told I don't give off the finest first impression, but I would really like it if we could be friends." She tucked her hair behind her ears. "You live in London too. We should go for cocktails at the races or see a show sometime?"

Well, that was unexpected. I looked for any sign of a punchline, but there didn't seem to be any. "I've never been to the races. To be honest with you, I don't feel right betting on the animals." Was that what she and Vicky did together, go to the horse races? I thought Vicky hated that kind of thing. Especially with Crystal being a rescue.

"We don't have to. I just…thought it might be nice."

Now I was feeling sorry for her. Dammit! It would be nice for Vicky if the two of us got along, after all. I should make the effort for her. I swallowed my pride. "I'm sure we can figure something out."

Tanya smiled. For a second I could see what Vicky might see in her, even if they did seem worlds apart. "Great. I'll sort it. It's so quiet here, isn't it? It'll be nice to do something fun."

Mistleberry was small, sure, but it was my home; I felt the need to defend it.

Before I could, she continued, "Please do consider coming to the party, though. I'd really like it if you were there."

Part of me didn't want to ask the question, but I had to. "How come?"

She glanced over her shoulder. "Well—and please keep this just between us—I'm planning a certain something, and I know it would mean a lot to her if you were there to celebrate with us."

A certain something? How wonderfully vague. I tried to stay cool and collected, but my stomach twisted, as though Tanya had reached inside and grabbed hold of my insides with her fist. "And what would that be?" I asked reluctantly.

Tanya's eyes held mine, daring me to look away. "I'm going to ask her to marry me. But please keep this just between us."

I didn't hear anything after "marry me". My heart fell out of my arse, my ears ringing with the thought of the two of them...together...forever. I swallowed, my mouth not wanting to speak the words.

"You're going to ask Vicky to marry you?" I asked quietly.

"Yes. And I want all her closest friends and family to be there so we can start the New Year with a bang." She smiled at me, and it took everything in me to force a smile back. "You can invite your girlfriend too, of course."

My girlfriend? My mind raced to catch up with itself. She had probably been spying on Katie earlier. "Isn't three months a bit fast?"

She shrugged off my comment. "All I can say is, when you know, you know. So, will you come?"

"I'm not sure. I might have...some...work stuff to do." I moved closer to my house, slipping on the ice but righting myself before I fell tits over arse. I waved away Tanya's attempts to help me. "I'll see you later. But congrats! I'm really...happy for you both. Okay, talk to you later!"

Before I could put any more of my foot in my mouth, I fell onto the front door, finding it locked. I fumbled in my pocket for my keys, my hands shaking as I tried to find the keyhole. *Vicky getting married?*

It was all over. It was done. And so was I. Done with

Mistleberry. Forget what I said. I needed to leave. I was out of here. I didn't know who I was trying to kid. I wasn't cut out for any of this.

There was only so much I could take—and maybe Katie was right. Me being here was just interfering with Vicky's life. What good would it do? It would only bring me pain while keeping her from moving on completely. We needed a clean cut.

Tears filled my eyes as I finally flung open the door, knocking into my aunt and uncle, who seemed equal parts perplexed and frightened to see me in such a state.

Without an apology—or any words at all—I sprinted upstairs to my room, avoiding Cameron's judging stare at me from the photos on the walls. I heaved my suitcase onto my bed and sobbed, tossing in my belongings through blurry vision.

I stopped to catch my breath, but the words rang inside my head, just like they did when I heard the news about Cameron.

I'm going to ask her to marry me.

I'm going to ask her to marry me.

Cameron's dead.

Cameron's dead.

It's over.

It's over.

Chapter Twenty-Seven

Nothing made any sense right now. The only thought I could hold on to was that it was time to go. Seeing Vicky and Tanya together was one thing, but having to witness their engagement and pretend to be happy for them was one step too far. I couldn't just sit back and let it all unfold around me. There was nothing more I could do. Vicky knew how I felt about her, and I wasn't about to go and declare why she should be with me and not Tanya. It wasn't my place. It was her decision; I needed to respect that. My only option was to leave.

The front door slammed, and Mum charged up the stairs, so easily recognisable by her loud stomping feet.

"Dad! You said you wouldn't call her!"

Dad shuffled into view from the hallway. "I'm sorry, love. I didn't know what to do." His sad puppy-dog eyes stabbed me with guilt. I was abandoning them again, running away.

"What's all this about, Holly? I've only nipped to the horse for five minutes and all hell breaks loose." Mum scanned the room with wide eyes before settling on me and softening. "Oh, honey. Come here." She pulled me into her embrace despite my reluctance, but once I breathed in that comforting smell, the tears wouldn't stop. I slumped into her shoulder.

"She's—going—marry—Tanya." I sniffed into her gilet, my chest heaving.

"Hang on a second. I can't understand a word you're saying." She rubbed a comforting hand over my back, reminding me of when I was a kid. "Take some deep breaths, love."

After a few minutes, I sighed and straightened, unable to look her in the eye. I picked a spot on the fading blue carpet and exhaled. "Vicky's going to marry Tanya. Tanya's going to propose to her at the New Year's party, and I…"

Tears spilled down my cheeks again, and Mum wiped them with her thumb.

The raw emotion on Mum's crumpled face told me she understood. I didn't have to explain any more. She pulled me back into her chest and wrapped her arms around me. "I'm sorry, love."

"Please don't hate me."

She grabbed my shoulders to look me in the eye. "Hate you? Why on earth would you say something like that?"

"For leaving you and Dad." I met his glassy eyes over Mum's shoulder. "For leaving again."

Mum shook her head. "I could never hate you, Holly. Not even if you hated me. Not even if you never came back to Mistleberry again." She gave me a small smile. "Not even if you ate the last custard cream."

I let out a soft laugh.

"We'd never hate you, Hol," Dad agreed from behind her.

Mum waved him forward, and he joined the hug. My parents were amazing. That thought just made me cry more.

"I will come back," I said. "I will. I just need some time to think about things. About what I want to do."

"That's okay, love. You need to look after yourself." Mum glanced at the suitcase on my bed. "Do you need any help?"

I shook my head. "I think I'm all set."

At the sound of three sharp knocks, we all swivelled our heads towards the door.

Something flashed across Mum's face, and she bit

her lip.

"What is it?" I asked.

"Well, when your dad called me, I was at the horses…with Vicky."

I groaned, pulled my hand through my hair, and wiped my tear-stained face.

"I can tell her to go," Dad suggested. Though the very thought of him trying to do so seemed absurd. He couldn't tell a ghost "boo".

"I can tell her, love," Mum said, picking up on my reluctance. "If that's what you want?"

Three more knocks.

My pulse skyrocketed, pounding in my neck. "It's okay. You can let her in."

"You sure?"

I nodded. She deserved to know. *Better do this quick—before I change my mind.*

My parents scuttled away, Mum to open the door and Dad to go hide in the living room. He wasn't a fan of confrontation; that was probably where I got it from.

I looked at myself in the mirror, dabbing at my red cheeks and bloodshot eyes. It was no use. There was no hiding my emotions this time. Muffled voices at the door turned into footsteps. Each step closer increased the thumping in my chest. Then the bedroom door opened.

Vicky tentatively stepped in, her hair curled loosely around her face. Those blue eagle eyes picked apart the organised mess in my room. Then her gaze fell on me.

"Holly, are you okay? What's wrong?" She closed the door behind her and moved into my eyeline, but I couldn't look at her. It made what I was about to say so much harder.

I scrunched my eyes closed, remembering Tanya's words. *I'm going to ask her to marry me.* "I'm going back to London."

"You are?" I could hear the confusion in her voice.

I was silent for a moment. I didn't know what to say.

"Why are you leaving?" she continued. "I thought you were staying for New Year?"

I picked up the dress I'd worn the night before and threw it in the suitcase. I could hear Dani in my head, cursing me for crumpling the expensive garment in such a way, but I didn't care. I stuffed in some pairs of socks and a handful of T-shirts that were stacked on my desk. "It's a work thing. I need to be back sooner than I thought."

"Before New Year?" The scepticism dripped from her words. Vicky tried to catch my eye, but I wouldn't let her.

"Something about a new product launch."

"You really think you can lie to me that easily, Holly? Especially with the way your mum panicked and ran back here like the world was falling off its axis." She grabbed my arm, and I bit back a gasp, dropping some socks on the floor. "Look me in the eyes and tell me that's really why you're going."

Heat surged through the places where our skin touched. My eyes were stinging as I tried to fight back the tears. But it was too late. "I'm sorry," I said. "But I have to go."

She took a step closer, her eyebrows pinching together. "Holly…what's wrong? Please, talk to me. I'm worried about you—"

"I can't do it, Vicky."

She paused, her gaze studying my face. "Can't do what?"

I swallowed, but the lump immediately reappeared in my throat. "I can't just be your friend right now."

Slowly, understanding rolled over her features, and then her own eyes glassed over. "Hol," she said, so quietly it was a whisper. Her bottom lip wobbled, and my heart cracked in two.

I wanted to wrap my arms around her; I wanted her to wrap hers around me. I wished with every cell in my body I could seal the two of us in a bubble and we could stay in our own little world. I'd known the holiday season couldn't last forever, but it felt like this feeling could have. For the first time, I *wanted* it to. I wasn't scared of our relationship or what it meant about my life. I wasn't afraid of the commitment or the change. I'd transfer offices and move up here to be with her. But none of that mattered, because she had Tanya. It was too little, too late, and I couldn't do anything about it.

"What changed?" Vicky asked.

I couldn't tell her about what Tanya said. As much as we didn't see eye to eye, it was unfair to ruin that moment for the two of them. I looked down at the floor. Vicky's eyes made me feel so many things I couldn't cope with. "I know my limit," I said. "I know what I can handle, and this…I just can't."

She nodded, then glanced about the room, exhaling hard and combing her hands through her hair. "Fuck." She spun back to me. "Is it selfish of me to not want you to go? 'Cos I don't want you to go."

The air in the room thickened, and heat pricked up my neck. "I don't know what else to do."

"Fuck. Fuck." She sat on the bed, sinking into the mattress. My suitcase slipped into her side, but she didn't seem to notice. "Are you going to come back?"

"I don't know my plans at the minute."

She shook her head. "Of course. I'm sorry. I just didn't expect you to leave so soon. I thought we'd have more time to talk."

"Say it now. What did you want to talk about?"

She looked up at me, snaring me in those blue eyes.

Say you want me. That you'll leave her. That you love me.

But she didn't. Vicky looked back at me silently,

while tears slipped down her cheeks. That told me everything I needed to know.

I needed to go. Mistleberry couldn't be my home, not while she was still here. My heart couldn't take it. It was time to close this chapter of my life and shut the door on us.

It was time to move on.

Chapter Twenty-Eight

Everything in my apartment was the same. The walls were still white, my clothes still hanging neatly in the wardrobe, my stack of work waiting for me on the dining table. Everything was the same, but I felt different, misplaced. I was the one who'd changed.

I didn't care about work, or climbing the ladder in Pertoni Clark's company. What I'd previously aimed towards and spent countless nights working on felt flat and meaningless. I'd tried to sift through some of the proposals for the New Year from the comfort of my bed, but my eyes glossed over the empty words. I just didn't care.

I cared about the love of my life, my first love, my best friend, about to become engaged to someone else. I'd spent the entire time since I'd got back in my pyjamas, sulking around my apartment and ignoring the rest of the outside world. I didn't want to think about Vicky and everything I'd left behind, but somehow that was all I could do. Sadness seeped into my pores, and memories of Cameron's death haunted me, prodding barely healed wounds. I'd not come out of my apartment for a week that time. The walls remembered that, mirrored that pain and reflected it back to me. My heart still ached when I thought of him. I knew it always would, but it was muted now, a soft ache that was sometimes more comforting than painful. Right now, my emotions all balled together into a big ball of gloom.

I missed Cameron. Finding and losing Vicky was something I'd not expected to have to deal with too. I knew I'd be okay. I'd bounce back. Just not now. Or tomorrow. Or in the New Year.

I wonder if Pertoni Clark is planning to expand to Italy? That might work.

Five loud knocks jolted me from my daydream. The neighbours were probably having a party.

More knocks.

I sighed. Did everyone have to be having the best time when I was going through a crisis? How insensitive of them.

"I know you're in there!"

The voice made me start. This couldn't be a police raid. Highly unlikely, anyway—unless they were on the lookout for a sad Mistleberry runaway who hadn't washed or left her bed since arriving back in London.

"Open up! Reinforcements are here!"

I groaned and rolled over, shoving a pillow over my head. The knocks thumped against the door in a constant rhythm, forcing me from my sad nest. *I'm going to kill her for this.* My feet dragged along the sleek floor towards the lunatic banging at my door.

Begrudgingly, I opened it. My best friend stood there, two huge bags full of shopping hanging off her arms. Before I could say anything, she barged past me, heaving it all onto the table.

"Thank god. These bags are so friggin' heavy. At least I don't have to feel bad about not going to the gym." She turned to me, her wild, black curls strewn about her face. She brushed her hair out of her eyes and then frowned when she saw me. "Oh, dear. Bring it in."

"Dani, I really just want—"

"Bring it in!" She opened her arms, and, with a sigh, I wrapped mine around her. Not that I would admit it, but I did feel a little better. She gave the cutest hugs because she was so small, allowing me to rest my head on top of hers. "I take it things with Bedroom Girl didn't go well?"

"No, they did not."

"I'm sorry, Hol. I'll be having words with Camille about this, don't worry."

"Phew. That was what I was worrying about, your psychic's reliability and reputation."

She squeezed me, then pulled back, tapping me lightly on the nose. "There she is. That snark is still there beneath the surface. This is fixable still, which is good." She dived into the shopping bags, barely able to see over the counter. "Now, what are you fancying? I've got everything. Ice cream, chocolate, those weird salt and vinegar nuts you like. Name it, I've got it."

"A mute button for yourself? Why are you so happy? Can't you just be miserable with me?"

"Nope. Sorry, I don't have that. Feel free to leave some feedback on Daniisthebestdotcom though." She flashed a smile at me and then produced a tub of ice cream from the depths of her bag. "Chocolate and honeycomb?"

"Fine," I grumbled and trailed my way back into my bedroom.

"Not so fast. I love you, I do, but I'm not joining you in your bed of doom. Let's set up on the sofa."

I narrowed my eyes at her. "I'm so glad you stopped by," I replied.

"Now, sit. Eat ice cream. Tell me everything. And I mean *everything*." Dani plopped herself down on my leather sofa and rested her feet on the coffee table. "Then you're going to have a shower, clean your sheets, and we'll have a nice quiet New Year watching films and eating rubbish. You'd better appreciate it too. I called off my diet for this. I've officially lost to Janet and Mina in the office."

The mention of New Year made me frown. I didn't know what time it was, but judging by the lack of light outside, it was edging closer to that moment. A knife twisted in my gut at the image of the two of them, celebrating and in love. Yuck. Gross. Ugh. I wanted my bed.

"What did I say?" Dani asked. "Why has your face got even sadder?"

Tears welled in my eyes, and I couldn't fight them. I thought I'd be all cried out by now. I sat next to her and let out a sob. Dani wrapped her arm around me, and I leaned into her.

"What about you and Brandon? I don't want to ruin your plans."

"Pssh. Brandon is fine. He's a big boy. You're more important."

I told her everything in between sobs, sharing laughs at the robot scarecrow for Harry, and at me falling off Vicky's horse. Dani listened as I spoke about our kiss on the Ferris wheel and the night in the hotel, plus how much I'd been struggling with Cameron's death.

She scraped the bottom of the ice-cream tub with the spoon. "And Katie didn't try and kill you or any of your family?"

"No, she actually apologised. We had a good talk. She said some things that actually resonated with me. And she just wanted some stuff of hers back."

"Wow. And people say that there's no such thing as Christmas miracles."

Afterwards, I showered and changed my bedding, already feeling a little lighter for sharing. I swiped open my phone, hoping for some sort of message, but I'd only received messages from Mum. I tried not to let the lack of contact get to me. I'd requested it, after all, but it still soured my stomach. I missed Vicky. Had Tanya already proposed?

"Hey! I told you, no looking at your phone." Dani plucked it out of my hands and laid it face-down on the bed.

"Sorry. I just…"

"I know, it's hard. But staring at your phone isn't going to make it better. Staring at the TV, though? That cute older actress you like?"

"I can't watch Carol right now," I grumbled. "No romance."

"Okay. Let's find a murder documentary."

We cuddled up on the sofa while Dani flicked through the options. I couldn't focus, and my mind continued to wander back to Mistleberry.

Maybe this was how it was supposed to be. There'd

always been a question mark above our heads. This could be the closure I needed for Vicky and me to be friends and stay that way. Without complications of love or sex, our foundation of friendship was still there. It might take time, but if Vicky was happy, I could let it go.

Maybe. I could try at least. I still needed her in my life.

Cheers and whistles echoed from next door, and a heavy bassline thumped through the walls. My neighbour Nick must've actually been having a party, after all.

We'd barely got through the opening credits when there was a knock at the door.

Dani glanced at me with her mouth pursed. "What? It's not me. I'm already here."

"Well, can't you get it?" I grumbled.

"Come on. This is a step in your rehabilitation. Freshly washed, check. No more chocolate-stained clothes, check. Time to interact with a real-life person now."

I scowled. "I'm interacting with you, aren't I?"

"Nuh-uh. Off you go."

I growled as she gave me a loving push off the sofa. I kicked the blanket off me and shuffled towards the door, stopping midway as a thought rushed into my head.

What if it was her?

Of course it isn't her. She doesn't even know where I live.

Vicky was probably three champagne glasses in, being cheered by her closest family and friends. She wouldn't be outside my door in London.

"That's good," Dani encouraged. "Now the other half of the way."

I closed my eyes, deciding not to waste my energy on giving her an exasperated look over my shoulder. I shuffled the last few steps and put my finger on the handle. The door swung open, and my heart dropped.

A part of me, somewhere deep down underneath all my logic and reason, had still hoped it would be Vicky.

"Hey, Holly, I, er…woah. Are you okay?" Nick's bushy eyebrows furrowed together as he took in my appearance. "I, er, I'm having a bit of a party over there, so if you fancy a drink or two and have nothing planned, feel free to come on over." He bobbed his head.

The silence stretched out, making both of us uncomfortable. I sighed, mustering all my strength to try and care even a little bit about his New Year's Eve party. The dude always left his rubbish bags in the hallway. It was super annoying. But the gesture was sweet, even if the invitation was probably a sorry attempt to sweet talk me into overlooking the loud music pumping from his apartment. "Thanks, Nick. Enjoy your night."

"Peace." He held up two fingers, twirled his moustache, and headed back across the hall.

I took a step back, letting my apartment door close—but someone stuck their foot inside, flinging it back open.

Chapter Twenty-Nine

Dani must have spiked the ice cream with something because my mind was projecting a delusion. A perfect blue-eyed hallucination of Vicky Castleton was standing outside my door. But on closer inspection, her eyes were red and bloodshot, her lovely mouth set in a frown.

I couldn't speak, afraid the sound of my own voice would dislodge the mirage. She looked me over, her expression not dissimilar to that of Nick's just moments ago.

"What's the hold-up?" Dani called from behind me. I heard her move across the floor towards us, but I was rooted to the spot. My mind couldn't comprehend why

Vicky would be here. If she was, did that mean…

"I broke up with Tanya."

The words struck my chest like an arrow. *Broke up. With Tanya.*

Vicky's attention flicked behind me, her eyes narrowing in question.

"I'm Dani. The best friend." Dani reached around me to shake Vicky's hand.

Vicky glanced at me before returning the gesture. "Vicky."

Dani squealed. "Bedroom Girl! I knew it. I knew it. Camille isn't losing her touch after all." She clapped her hands together, ignoring the glare I was aiming her way, then cleared her throat. "Well! It's clear you two have some talking to do. So I'll get out of your hair." She ducked back into my apartment, picked up her handbag, car keys, and the share bag of Maltesers, and joined us back in the hallway. She kissed me on the cheek. "Call me if you need anything, okay?"

I nodded. "Thank you."

The whirlwind that was my best friend descended the stairs, leaving me and a befuddled Vicky in the strange comfort of Nick's thumping music.

"So…are you going to invite me in?" Vicky asked.

"Oh. Yeah. Of course. Come in." I moved aside, hoping Dani had moved the gigantic pile of tissues I'd left by the bed. Oh god. Oh god. This was not how I imagined bringing Vicky Castleton back to my apartment. My sadness was strewn all over in the form of clothes and empty tubs of junk food.

She took in the space, her eyes lingering on the mess on the kitchen counters before switching to my bedroom door. She turned to me. "It's a really nice place."

"Thank you, but...I don't think you're here to browse London real estate, are you?"

She sighed. "No. No, I'm not." She paced the floor around the kitchen counter, mumbling to herself.

"What happened? Are you okay?"

She stopped pacing and combed a hand through her hair. "You happened, Holly. You in all your confusing and wonderful mystery. You already knew, didn't you?"

I blinked. "Knew what?"

She took a few steps towards me, and my heart stuttered in my chest, her sweet perfume making me dizzy. "That she was going to propose to me."

I exhaled. "She might have mentioned it, yeah."

Vicky gave me a sad smile. "Why didn't you say anything?"

"It wasn't my place. I'd already overstepped the mark...and you deserve to be happy, Vicky. You really do."

"I think so too. And that's why I'm here." She lifted her eyes to meet mine. "I hated seeing you with Katie. I was surprised by how jealous I was, and it brought back all those feelings from before. It broke my heart watching you leave again, seeing you hurting so badly. I wanted to talk to you about it. I thought we'd have more time but...I don't want to let the fear win. I don't want us to keep breaking each other's hearts." She took another step towards me. "You leaving again made me realise just how much you make my life better, Hol. You're silly and clumsy and funny and so..." She grinned, and my heart squeezed. "So confusing. And hot. I hate to admit it, to make that head of yours any bigger, but it's true. I'd already got this life planned out, this idea of what would make me happy, but it wasn't it. It was a lie. Seeing you with your ex made me realise I couldn't do that again."

I swallowed. "What are you saying?"

"That, not for the first time, you've well and truly snared my heart, Holly Bradfield."

My ears heard the words, but I couldn't comprehend them. I'd just come to terms with losing her again, with the idea of moving on, and my mind wouldn't let the wall down. I couldn't deal with the hurt again, couldn't bear for it to be ripped away so soon. I couldn't handle it.

"What about Tanya?" I asked.

"It's over. We weren't right for each other. She knew it too, really. I think she proposed just because she didn't want to lose me. But it felt...forced." She cupped my cheek with her hand. "What's going on in there? Talk to me."

Tears filled my eyes, and I couldn't wash them away. Vicky brushed the strays with her fingertips. So gentle. So perfect. Too good for me.

"I'm scared," I admitted. "I can't…"

"Can't what?"

"Lose you again."

"What makes you think that you will?"

"Because look at us. It's already happened twice."

She brushed the tears from my face, her fingertips caressing my cheek and down to my jawline. "Why is it that we are always so afraid to go after what we want?"

My mind was too full, crammed with thoughts all fighting for attention. Self-sabotage? It seemed easier that way. I shook my head, forcing myself to meet Vicky's gaze, which penetrated the steel armour I'd forced back around my heart. Those kind eyes that had known me and loved me for so much of my life. The eyes that made me feel so much, sometimes it was hard to bear I sucked in a deep breath, letting it steady the unease pulsing through me. "Because what we really want has the most power to truly hurt us. The most risk."

Vicky nodded, her eyes shimmering. "The most risk, but also the most reward." She took a step towards me. "I couldn't live with the what-if, Hol. Not again. I don't want to run either. I want you."

"You do? You want me?"

She placed her hand behind my neck, angling my

face to look at her. "Yes. Why is that so hard for you to believe?"

"Because you're you. And I'm me. And there's Tanya…"

"It's over. I couldn't be with her and claim to give her everything when my heart is already with you. It always has been."

My eyes met hers. I wanted to believe her. But this seemed too good to be true. Things like this didn't happen to me without a catch. I needed to read the fine print. The clause that said "however, this happiness will only last until the clock strikes midnight". To locate the trapdoor before I fell through and broke my legs.

"I know you're scared," Vicky said. "I am too. But for this to work, you need to trust me."

I swallowed, afraid to ask the question. "Do you trust me?"

"Yes," she answered immediately.

Relief shot into my chest. "What changed?"

"We talked. You opened up. I can understand more now, and we can learn from our mistakes. When I look into your eyes…I see it there. I see you." Her eyes watered, her gaze wandered over my face. "Do you trust me?"

Vicky had always been there for me. Even when I didn't offer her the same courtesy. She was kind, caring, funny, and extremely attractive. I trusted her like my family. Did that mean I could guarantee that she wouldn't hurt me? No. Nobody could give me that. I'd hurt her too, when that was the last thing I'd ever wanted to do. But her word, that was something I had full belief in. She probably knew me better than I knew myself.

"I do," I said softly, tears pricking my eyelids. Everything had changed so fast, and yet, had also taken so long. I knew Cameron would've been cheering for us all the time. Just like Dani and her psychic.

"Then let me show you." Vicky leaned in and kissed me, taking the breath from my lungs.

I grasped at her coat, melting into her kiss.

Something stirred low in my belly. Emotions that I'd tried to keep dormant for what felt like an eternity sprung to the surface.

Her hands roamed my back, caressing my curves and gripping my waist. *Vicky's hands are on my waist. Is this happening?* A shot of arousal flooded my core, and I kissed her harder, leading her to my bedroom.

I kicked open the door, crashing it against the wall, but I didn't care. The only thing I cared about was the taste of Vicky on my lips. Why hadn't we done this before? How had this taken us so long?

She slipped her tongue into my mouth, and I groaned, my belly turning into putty.

I pushed her back onto my bed, and we finally broke apart, gasping for air. Vicky's eyes were a hooded, darkened blue. I'd never seen her look this way before.

I swallowed, my chest heaving and my mind struggling to keep up with everything. "I can't believe you're here."

That wasn't sexy. Come on, Holly. Get a grip.

"I've thought about you a lot in this room," I said.

"You have?" Vicky seemed surprised.

I nodded. "I used to fantasise about what might happen if we were to run into each other in London."

Her cheeks flushed pink, but her face fell serious. "Are you going to show me?"

"Yes." Before my nerves could take hold of me, I pulled my T-shirt over and off my head and let it fall to the floor. Vicky's attention dropped to my bare chest.

"Wow. I can't believe I'm looking at Holly Bradfield naked."

"Don't full name me. That's weird." I slid towards her, and she leaned back on her elbows, allowing me to climb on top of her.

She let out a soft laugh. "Sorry. But you're just...wow." She sat up, planting kisses on my stomach and taking a nipple into her mouth. Her hot tongue caressed it gently, pulling at my abdomen. I tangled my fingers in her hair and tugged lightly. Her teeth grazed my nipple in response, making me buck my hips against her.

I pulled back to unzip her coat, sliding it off her arms and throwing it onto my chair, quickly followed by her T-shirt and then her bra.

Vicky's eyebrows bounced. "I want to tease you about the speed with which you did that, but honestly, I am a little impressed."

"You always want to tease me about something." I kissed her again, softly this time, letting our lips do the talking.

Warmth spread through me to the tips of my fingertips. Kissing Vicky Castleton was fucking amazing.

I straddled her, and Vicky pulled her focus up to meet my gaze. Something hidden in her eyes made me pause.

"Are you nervous?" I asked.

"Of course I am. This is you we're talking about. This is a serious line to cross."

"We don't have to do anything if you don't want to. There's no rush."

She smiled, shaking her head a little. "I've waited for this for…about thirteen years. Stop overthinking and just kiss me."

I pushed her down on the bed, and she gasped. A surge of confidence pulsed through me, encouraged by her reaction. I wanted to hear more. I wanted to hear everything.

I kissed her, savouring every moment. Electric heat surged through my veins, demanding friction in my lower half. But I didn't want to stop kissing her.

Our kisses grew more frantic, wandering hands and hungry mouths fighting for attention. I felt Vicky's hand rub me through my pyjama bottoms, and everything went white for a moment. *Holy hell.*

She grabbed the waistband and tried to tug them off. I adjusted myself and tore them down my legs, kicking them off the bed. We fell back together, exploring each other like desperate teenagers. Those parts of us that we'd tried to deny for so long were finally taking centre stage, and no scared adult was going to tell them to stop.

I popped open the button on Vicky's jeans, sliding down the zipper and slipping my hand inside. Her wetness slicked my fingers even through the material of her pants, and I groaned into her mouth. I made slow circles, and Vicky pushed herself into me, letting out a soft gasp. Delicious desire coiled in my belly. The jeans were too restrictive; they needed to go.

I pulled back to remove them, caught momentarily by the look in Vicky's eyes. The want. The need.

I couldn't get back to her quickly enough.

I kissed her, hooking my arm behind her back so I could move us up the bed. I had a taste of how wet she was, and I couldn't wait any longer. My fingers found her opening, and I glided inside.

Vicky arched back on the bed, and I swallowed her moans with my kiss as I worked inside her. She dug her nails into my back, sending flurries of goose bumps over my body.

"Oh my god, Holly."

My stomach somersaulted hearing my name in her mouth. It was the hottest thing I'd ever heard.

She reached for me, sucking on my lip and brushing our tongues together. The touch sent a direct wave between my legs, and I almost lost my concentration. I fucked her harder, soaking up every sound, wanting this moment to last forever.

Her legs started quivering, her breathing rasped as she got closer.

She fluttered her eyes open, sucking me into that pool of blue.

"You're going to make me cum," she whispered. No sooner had the words left her mouth than her legs convulsed, her hand fisting into my hair. I watched as she rode out the waves, burning every sensation into my memory so I could relive it again and again.

Everything felt right. Like we'd been doing this forever.

I kissed her again, slow, our lips barely touching. I brushed my lips along her jaw to her neck, planting soft kisses to the dip behind her collarbone.

"Mmm. You're setting me off again," Vicky murmured, her voice low in her throat.

"Already? Wow, someone's insatiable," I teased.

"It's you. You're just too hot."

I pulled back, a smile tugging at my mouth. "And you're in a delusional post-orgasmic haze."

She shook her head, her blue eyes sparkling. "I'm not. I've always thought that about you."

"Is that so?"

She swatted me playfully. "Don't be an arse."

Pulling me close, she ran her hands up my back. I adjusted myself so that our legs slid together and pushed against her.

She gasped.

My eyes rolled back at the glorious feel of her hot and wet against me. "Holy hell," I muttered, positioning myself above her to grab the headboard. I angled my hips, grinding against her. Pleasure rolled through my core, and I increased the pace.

Vicky kissed me, her tongue gliding against mine like silk. A jolt of ecstasy shot through my abdomen. I couldn't keep quiet, it felt too good.

"I like hearing you," she whispered against my lips. "I'd wondered about that too."

My breathing quickened, and I felt release building in my centre. Reading my mind, she gripped my waist, flipping me onto my back.

"Not yet, you don't."

I missed the contact instantly. I could feel myself throbbing and moved my hand to fulfil the ache. Vicky watched as I worked circles over myself, feeling myself pulse more under her gaze.

She lowered herself onto the bed and scooted back, holding my eye contact the entire time. Strong hands gripped my thighs and spread them, exposing me completely to her.

Wow. Vicky Castleton's face is between my legs.

She wet her lips, then in a quick movement, pulled me towards her, sinking her tongue into me.

I groaned as she pushed deeper, flicking up into a sensitive spot. All sense of self vanished as she turned her attention to my throbbing clit, swirling her tongue in delicious circles. I was close. So close to finishing right there on her tongue.

I squirmed underneath her, completely at her mercy. Then her fingers teased at my entrance, slicking up and down in my wetness. She pulled up from my legs to meet my eye, giving me no chance to catch my breath before she thrust into me.

Her hot mouth sucked back onto my clit, her fingers pushing me further and further towards the edge. My grip tightened on her hair as the gravitational pull in my core intensified, filling me with red-hot euphoria spilling out all over.

With a guttural moan, I climaxed, legs shuddering as Vicky squeezed every last wave of pleasure out of me. I gasped when she removed her fingers, but her tongue still pressed against me, her warm breath heightening every nerve ending. With a gentle sweep, she kissed me once more, making me flinch, and pushed herself onto her elbows.

Still lost in the highs of orgasm, my eyes found hers. An overwhelming sense of love washed over me, drowning me in her soft blue irises. She was the whole package. I couldn't believe how stupid I was to nearly let her walk away.

"I can't believe you're here," I said again.

She smiled. "I know. I can't believe it either."

"But I'm very happy you are."

"Who's in a delusional post-orgasmic haze now?" she teased.

"Shut up, and come here."

She crawled up the bed and collapsed beside me, wrapping her arm around my waist. I looped my leg over hers and sighed. Everything felt right with our bodies so close, skin to skin. I kissed her shoulder, and she giggled, lighting a fire in my chest.

She's so adorable.

The background noise filtered back in, the cheering and hollering mixed with loud indecipherable music. Fireworks exploded outside the window, casting orange and green sparkles across the night sky. Rockets whistled up into the blackness, exploding into colourful twisting swirls.

"You have such an amazing view of the city here,"

Vicky said, snuggling closer into my chest.

And the perfect person now to share that with.

"What?" Vicky turned her head to me.

Did I just say that out loud? Please don't tell me I said that out loud. Oh, god.

"Nothing," I mumbled.

She chuckled. "I can't wait to tell your mother what a soppy sod you are."

"You wouldn't dare." I tickled her lower back, and she shrieked, arching away from me.

"Stop! Not fair." She jutted me in the ribs. "No tickling me after sex."

I smiled. "I think I can live with that."

More fireworks shot into the night sky, raining the city with beautiful purples, oranges, and greens. I glanced at the clock on the bedside table. 12:03.

The happiness had lasted past midnight. Perhaps I'd finally broken the spell—or stopped worrying about ghosts of my past chasing me. I wanted to be in the moment. To soak up every minute of it with her.

"Happy New Year, Vicky," I whispered.

"Happy New Year, Hol." And she kissed me, filling my entire soul with light.

Epilogue

One Year Later

Not even a pigeon shitting on my favourite coat could dampen my spirits today. Driving back to Mistleberry wasn't just about visiting my home town for Christmas. This time, I was going home for good. Loaded with the last of my boxes in the car, and with Vicky's hand in my lap, we hurtled up the M1 towards our new start. Together.

Pertoni Clark had agreed to facilitate a move back up North. Most meetings could be done online or over the phone, with the agreement to attend one monthly meeting in person. Vicky planned to expand her mum's business ventures, deciding to trust her gut. I'd helped her with a business plan, and some colleagues at work had agreed to look over her proposal too. It was cute to see her so excited about it.

My therapist was helping me work through my grief, and Katie had been right, it was helping a lot. I was still a work in progress, but I was more than happy with that.

The country lanes greeted us with open arms, their familiar curves and bends a comfort instead of a hassle. I passed the park where the three of us used to hang out as kids, remembering Cameron and letting the memory warm those spaces in my heart. We drove past our parents' street, laughing about how our mothers had insisted we try and rent a place on the same road.

I loved my mum and dad. But absolutely no chance.

We wound through the next town, passing the turn for Donnington and the disaster that was the ice fair. A lot of things about that night had changed me, though. I guessed I had the blizzard to thank for that. It'd made me realise just how important Vicky was to me. We'd vowed to go back to the ice fair this year, and actually go ice-skating this time. Cameron would've teased me endlessly about how soppy I'd become—but I didn't even care. Instead of the idea making me sad, I smiled. He'd always be in my thoughts, and he'd always be my brother. I could never run away from that—I wouldn't want to.

Finally, we pulled onto the drive of our new home, a small two-bedroom house by the river. We'd come there as kids, the three of us racing boats down the river and swimming in the water on hot days. Back when our biggest concern was who could jump the furthest and what our parents would make us for tea. We'd no idea about the future; all that mattered was the three of us. How the bonds we made would last a whole lifetime. People might grow and change or leave, but the memories would live on forever.

"Home, sweet home," Vicky commented, exiting the car and looking up at our house.

I joined her, wrapping an arm around her waist as she kissed my temple. "Long time coming."

"Yeah, 'bout time you realised what a catch I am," she teased.

"Well, now you're hooked, there's no turning back."

"Hooked, huh? Someone thinks highly of themselves."

"I do after last night." I raised my eyebrows pointedly.

"Hey!" Vicky's face flushed red, and she pinched me. "You promised not to say anything."

"There's no one here. And female ejaculation is nothing to be ashamed of."

"Holly!" she hissed. "The neighbours might hear you."

"Pssh. All right. Can you help me with these boxes, please, oh Greatest-Catch-of-Them-All?" I started towards the boot, but she grabbed my arm.

"I mean, it's not the worst thing you've ever called me." She leaned her head towards the door. "Let's get the boxes after. I wanna show you something first."

Twice in one day? It isn't even my birthday. "Okay, sure."

She shook her head at me, leading us towards the door. "You've got a one-track mind, woman. Come on."

"I don't know what you're talking about."

She gave me a look over her shoulder and laughed. "Sure you don't." She handed me the key. "Want to do the honours?"

I took the key from her and slotted it in the lock, giving her a quick kiss before turning it and pushing the door. I was eager to jump into this new start with both feet.

The door swung open, and instead of being pushed against the wall and ravaged as I'd hoped, a barrage of voices calling "surprise!" almost barrelled me over.

"Fucking hell!" I clasped a hand to my chest before being tackled to the floor and screamed as the attacker pinned me down and licked my face. Barbaric! *Hang on a minute.* I tried to right myself, but the furry beast was too excited to see me.

"Butterbee, stop. I love you too, but—" I broke out laughing while someone pulled her off me.

With the blonde ball of fur out of my face, the rest of

the room came into focus. Dozens of smiling faces looked back at me, knocking me momentarily. All my favourite people in the world were here: Mum, Dad, Dani, Vicky's parents, Mr Simon. Even Harry waved from the corner of the now very cramped living room. Light reflected off the person next to him, except it wasn't a person at all. What the hell was Victrolly doing in my house? Wearing tinsel and a red Santa hat?

Mum rushed at me with the same enthusiasm as Butterbee, engulfing me in a hug. "Welcome home, love!"

"What is all this?" I asked, choking on her rose-scented perfume.

"It's your welcome home party. It's not every day your daughter comes back. We can see each other every day now. You can help me with the horses and we can make dinner. We can even…"

Oh, sweet lord. What have I done?

"Back off, Trace. You're going to scare her away again." Dad came to the rescue, putting a big arm around my shoulder.

I leaned into him, taking comfort in his embrace as the rest of the guests took their turns to welcome me back to Mistleberry.

"It's not technically Mistleberry," Mr Simon said, after patiently waiting his turn, "according to the border jurisdiction. But it's close enough." He looked sharp in a perfectly ironed navy-and-grey plaid shirt, dress trousers, and a black cardigan. Even his hair had been combed and his beard freshly trimmed.

I grinned. The amount of effort he'd put in made my stomach feel all soft. "Hey, Jeff. You scrub up well, don't you?"

He glanced down, giving a small smile. "Well, I thought it best to make an effort."

Adorable. So very adorable.

"How's Mabel?"

His face broke into a toothy grin. There was always one sure way to get Mr Simon to smile, and that was mention of his ginger cat.

"She had a very good breakfast this morning, her favourite tuna mixed with…"

Only once he was off, it was very hard to rein him back in. I nodded along as he explained Mabel's seven favourite foods—and not for the first time, either.

"This place is b-e-a-utiful!" my best friend enthused from the right. I could usually hear her before I could see her. I turned to catch her standing on her tiptoes, running her hand along the wooden mantelpiece and speaking to my aunt and uncle.

"It's so nice to have you back, dear." I spun round to the voice speaking, and Mrs Booth, the neighbour from four doors down, beamed back at me. "It is cold in here, though, isn't it?"

"Here. Take this, Marianne." Mr Simon shimmied

out of his black cardigan and draped it over her.

My mouth almost fell off. What's going on here then?

"Thanks, Jeffybear."

Jeffybear?

Either I was dreaming, had been transported to an alternative universe, or Mrs Booth had just called Mr Simon *Jeffybear*.

Mum called that there was cake in the kitchen, and I watched as the two of them hurried off together, not missing Jeff's hand on Marianne's lower back. *Well, I'll be damned.*

I looked around my new home, and emotion swelled inside me, warming my chest. All these people had turned out to celebrate us. *Dammit. Being in touch with my emotions now is so inconvenient.* But it felt so good to just let myself *feel.*

Vicky caught my eye from across the room, and my heart squeezed. She walked over to me, a grin that showcased her dimples stretched across her face. "Surprised?"

"Very." I looped my arm around her back and squeezed her to me. "Who's to blame for this, then?"

"Your mum. Definitely." She nodded to the stairs behind me. "My idea of welcoming you home is much more in line with your way of thinking." Her eyes found mine again, sparkling with mischief. Her slow smile made my insides twist, remembering how our bodies had been entwined just hours ago. I wondered if I'd ever be satisfied with touching her; I couldn't get enough of the feel of her skin on mine. We'd thirteen years to make up for, after all.

"Get outta here, you furry little maggots!"

Our attention was drawn by the screams behind us as Victrolly whirled its arms in circles, red lights flashing across its chest.

"Off, Victrolly. Turn off, girl!" Harry said, trying to restrain it, but the tin can was having none of it.

My stomach plummeted. This was going to be bad. I swear Mr Clark programmed mischief into his products; it was no coincidence that ninety percent of his inventions had a mind of their own. That man loved unpredictability and bedlam.

Victrolly grumbled and growled as she fought off Harry's attempts to control her. The guests backed away, murmuring concerns about why there was a robot scarecrow in the living room, and why it was growing more and more inconsolable.

"Is that supposed to happen?" Vicky whispered in my ear.

"No. No, it's not. Why did Harry bring that thing, anyway?"

"He thought it would be funny to reacquaint you with your old friend. Apparently he takes it everywhere."

Victrolly jerked out of Harry's grip and flew towards the nearest group of people, swirling her arms in vicious loops. They screamed and ran for the kitchen, where Mum shooed them out the back door and into the garden.

Dani shot me a look before running after the runaway robot. We'd been on the receiving end of many inventions gone wrong in the office.

"Leave now, before I get my shotgun!" Harry's voice boomed through Victrolly's speakers and another scream ripped through the room as people evacuated the house. The robot tore down the 'Welcome Home' banner and ripped it to shreds, muttering something about nests as it spun in erratic circles.

"A little help here!" Dani shouted as the scarecrow focused its attention on her and narrowly missed slamming into the coffee table.

Vicky kissed my cheek before offering her help. All I could do was laugh as the three of them tried to pin Victrolly into a corner. I supposed I should do something too, but the scene unravelling into utter disorder felt like the most perfect welcome home I could've imagined. Mistleberry was full of surprises.

I laughed louder, knowing Cameron was observing from somewhere, absolutely loving the show we were putting on for him. I glanced at his picture, propped up against the side-table, waiting to be hung up. I wanted to see him every day. I suppose I'd taken inspiration from

Mum's enormous jumble of photos on the stairs. I understood better now. I couldn't change the past, but I could remember it and use those memories to keep my brother alive in my future.

Victrolly screamed, its head dropped forward, and everything fell silent.

Harry turned to me, wide-eyed, chest heaving. But it wasn't over yet. A shrill sequence of beeps rumbled from the robot's centre, like the squawking of an old dial-up modem, and the head spontaneously burst into flames. Vicky grabbed the extinguisher from the kitchen and doused the manic robot in foam. The four of us glanced at each other, completely stunned. Then we cracked out into laughter.

Mistleberry was definitely full of surprises. Life was too. And if anyone had tried to tell me I'd spend my welcome home party watching my beautiful girlfriend and best friend trying to stop a robot scarecrow from destroying my living room, I'd have thought they were crackers—and for good reason. But even amid the chaos, there was nowhere else I'd rather be.

I was finally home, and not just for Christmas, but for good.

If you enjoyed this story, please do leave a review and let me know. Reviews and sharing/engaging on social media really make such a huge difference to indie authors like myself. The more support we get, the more novels we can write, and the more books there will be to read! If you got this far, I'm so humbled by your support, thank you.

Acknowledgments

Thank you so much for reading! I hope you enjoyed Holly and Vicky's story. I've wanted to write a sapphic Christmas book for a while now, and once I got the idea about Holly in my head, I couldn't shake it off. Grief can be overpowering at Christmas. I wanted to give Holly lots of love and a touch of silliness to reignite that hope that life can go on. For anyone reading this that's lost someone, I'm sending you love. You're not alone.

This story wouldn't be where it is today without my wonderful beta readers and editor Helena—thank you so much for all your input and hard work. Another big thank you to my ARC team! Your enthusiasm and excitement means so much to me, thank you for your help releasing my first ever self-published book! A huge thank you to all the lovely people for supporting me on Patreon too. I love being able to share my WIPs with you. Your encouragement keeps me going on the tough days. An extra special mention to Marie and Josh for being Sapphic champions of the world! You are the best. There are no words to express how much I value you. Thank you, thank you, thank you. Every like and comment and read means the world. I really appreciate your friendship.

The story I wrote on Patreon—*That Secret Something*—will be released in March and is now available for preorder! Here's the working blurb:

Rebecca Lawson is off-limits.

Jess knows this, but her best friend's devastatingly beautiful sister has snared her heart for as long as she can remember. She's sporty, tall, and confident—a lot of the things that Jess is not—but she's Lily's sister.

Nothing can ever happen between them.

Especially after that slip up at prom night.

But when Lily announces her engagement, and Jess and Rebecca are forced to spend time together planning the wedding, the heat rises and sparks fly. Amidst the chaos of raging bridezillas and other nuptial mishaps, can Jess resist temptation for the sake of her friendship?

Or will pursuing Rebecca Lawson break her heart?

My next WIP will be uploaded to Patreon weekly, along with some other fun benefits. If you're interested in checking it out and joining the club, my username is @emilywrightwriter.

Thank you to my girlfriend, Laura for putting up with all my blabbering and panics and late night stresses. I couldn't do this without you.

Last but not least, thank you, lovely reader, for taking the time to check out my story. Thank you so much for your support, you're making dreams come true.

Em x

About the Author

Emily Wright is a dog-loving, book-sniffing, ukulele-playing author who lives in Sheffield in the UK. When she isn't attached to her computer writing, she loves the outdoors, especially the crash of the ocean, the smell of pine, and starry night skies that make her feel absolutely obsolete. When not drinking tea and eating an unthinkable amount of Bourbons, she spends the rest of her time chasing her two naughty Spaniels around the house to stop them from eating anything and everything.

Connect with Emily here:
Website: www.emilywrightwriter.co.uk
Instagram: @emilywrightwriter
Patreon: @emilywrightwriter
Tiktok: @emilywrightwriter
Twitter: @emziewriter

Don't forget to subscribe to my newsletter to stay in touch and also receive a free sapphic novella, *All Bets Are Off*!

Abby Turner doesn't do relationships—she's very clear about that—yet, Sophia, her latest fling, obviously never got the memo. So, when a hot new woman moves into their business complex, both are eager to make a good first impression, and they strike up a bet: the first to win the new girl's heart. Abby's never said no to competition before, but there's something about new girl Gemma that leaves Abby with sweaty palms and the promise of trouble…

www.emilywrightwriter.co.uk/contact

Printed in Great Britain
by Amazon